D1525493

THE
THIEF

PETER O'MAHONEY

ALSO BY PETER O'MAHONEY

In the Jack Valentine Mystery Series:

Gates of Power
The Hostage
The Shooter
The Witness

*****

In the Tex Hunter Legal Thriller series:

Power and Justice
Faith and Justice
Corrupt Justice
Deadly Justice
Saving Justice
Natural Justice
Freedom and Justice
Losing Justice
Failing Justice

*****

In the Joe Hennessy Legal Thriller series:

The Southern Lawyer
The Southern Criminal
The Southern Killer

THE THIEF

JACK VALENTINE SERIES

BOOK 4

PETER O'MAHONEY

The Thief: A Gripping Crime Mystery
Jack Valentine 4

Peter O'Mahoney

Copyright © 2021
Published by Roam Free Publishing.
peteromahoney.com

1st edition.

Cover design by Belu.
https://belu.design

CHAPTER 1

THERE'S NOTHING final about death.

It's an ending, a finish, a completion of a journey, but final? No, I don't think so. There's nothing final about the heartache, there's nothing final about the memories that endure, and there's nothing final about the grief that burns your stomach every time a reminder crosses your path. A closing of a chapter, yes, but final? Not even close.

I watched Casey May, the partner in my investigation firm, wipe another tear from her eye as one of her friends shared a memory about her foster-brother, Rhys Mather. Memorials had a way of opening old wounds and bringing out suppressed emotions, allowing them to bubble to the surface, exposing them for the world to see.

"I remember the time we were late for baseball practice," the speaker said, looking down to the floor. "And the coach yelled at him, 'You're late! You should've been here at 5:30!' So Rhys turns to him and says, 'Why? Did something special happen at 5:30?' We had to run a lot of laps that day."

Casey May laughed with the other mourners, doing her best to control the raw emotion that was waiting just beneath her forced smile. If given a chance, her suppressed emotion would come charging forward, and there'd be no way she'd be able to control it.

The suburban yard was lit by the intermittent flickers of flames, dancing one direction and then the next, providing snapshots of the attendees' sad faces. The fifteen attendees were gathered around the fire pit, sitting on anything available—some were on camping chairs, others on milk crates, some rested on the back porch at the rear of the home. The smell of smoke from the fire was strong, but nobody was moving.

I scanned the yard as most of the people simply stared into their drinks, trying to counter the sentiment that always seemed to take hold in moments like this. Everybody's eyes were focused down, all except one pair. One pair of cold, dead eyes. The man sitting at the far end of the yard was looking at me. I knew of him. Mark Costa. A former baseball teammate of Rhys's, and now a rich property developer in Chicago. A big-hitter. A well-known prick. And most likely, a very corrupt human being. Costa wore plain black slacks and a white shirt with the sleeves rolled up, showing off a thick gold Rolex. His black hair was slicked back, there were bags under his eyes, and his jawline was clenched.

I held my gaze on him, and for a long moment, he returned the stare. He then turned back to the speaker, but his expressions remained blank. I wasn't going to confront him for staring at me, not here, and not today. I wasn't there to start a fight—I was there to support Casey; to be the stoic emotional rock she could lean on. Over the years Casey and I had worked together, I'd call her a friend more than a colleague. She knew me better than just about anyone else.

"The coach made us run laps for hours every time

Rhys tried to make a joke. He was always the joker," the speaker continued, and everyone chuckled. Of course, they did. Anything to avoid the melancholic emotions that were continuing to build.

Casey looked up and our eyes met. I could tell she knew what I was thinking—that I wanted to get out of there. She could read the guilt on my face as easily as I was reading the grief on hers. The moment seemed frozen as the guilt burned into me and yet, I could see something else in her eyes, something I didn't recognize at first. Her eyes turned back to the speaker, continuing to listen to the old war story that would no doubt end with another uncomfortable chuckle from the crowd. Moments later, it did just that.

I looked down at my beer, wishing I had chosen the whiskey instead. Whiskey was always better in these situations because the burn had a way of dulling the pain. But despite taking a quick glance at the bottle still sitting over on the table, I gripped the beer a little tighter.

Casey and her sister had grown up in various foster homes, and Rhys had been in-and-out of the same ones. He was the closest she'd ever had to a real brother, and she never referred to him as anything other than a brother. When Rhys's life was cut short the week before his first Triple-A minor league baseball start, she'd lost one of the few people she considered family. Rhys had died after hitting his head on the sidewalk late one night after being out drinking. They didn't find his body until the next morning, and by then, it was too late. A true tragedy for someone only twenty-five years old at the time, and even though ten years had passed, the tragedy didn't seem any less significant.

It'd been a long evening of stories, remembering a life that was cut short in its prime. I knew their pain, but my anguish came from a different tragedy. I'd lost my wife four years earlier in a school shooting, and anytime I was confronted with someone else's grief, my thoughts turned to her. She was an elementary school teacher—a caring, loving soul—and one of the many people that were shot that day.

It wasn't until the speaker finally paused long enough for someone else to speak that Casey intervened and asked for a final toast to the memories that had been shared for their friend. Casey raised her glass. She spoke a single word, then took a sip.

"Rhys," the rest of the group spoke in unison, rising out of their seats and taking a last drink from their chosen beverages.

Casey began to hug and thank the people closest to her, which was my signal to get out of there. I shot Casey a quick wink when our eyes briefly met. That was the good thing about having a partner you could rely on—sometimes, words weren't needed when trying to relay something emotional.

"Thanks for coming," Casey walked over and lowered her voice to almost a whisper. "I know it must be difficult with the memories of Claire and—"

I held up a hand and nodded. Casey took the hint and smiled. She opted for a hug, and I returned it. It was brief but held enough comfort for both of us. I'd never been much of a hugging guy, but if a hug was the polite way to stop her from mentioning my own grief, then a hug was what I would offer.

"I've always got your back," I rested my hand on her shoulder. "I'll see you in the morning."

I walked through the side gate of the yard, swinging it shut behind me. I pulled my coat tighter as I stepped out onto the front lawn, fishing for a smoke inside my coat. Despite having quit many times, there were moments I needed a cigarette, and after digging in my pocket, I found a squashed pack. As I went hunting for a way to light the dirty thing, I heard the familiar flick sound of a lighter behind me, and when I turned, I saw Mark Costa standing there, his own smoke already lit, with the lighter flame ready to light mine.

I chased the flame and gave him a gruff thanks as he flicked the lighter closed. He took a puff and held out his hand.

"Mark Costa."

I nodded, took a deep drag, and shook with him. "Jack—"

"Valentine, the Private Investigator. I know."

He finished the introduction for me, as if I somehow needed help remembering my own name.

"I quit a while ago," I said, looking at the end of the cigarette. "But times like this, the need just comes back."

"I've quit many times as well, but I…" he shrugged and stepped closer to me. "I knew Rhys better than most people."

He spoke with a low tone, almost like he was auditioning for a role in an action movie. I figured it was time to move on, but as I began to turn away, he reached out and grabbed my arm. It was then that I knew I definitely didn't like him.

I looked down at his hand still holding my arm, raised my eyebrows, and he let go, proving he wasn't quite as dumb as I'd first thought.

I didn't respond, and when he saw that I had no intention of furthering the conversation, he continued anyway. "I need your help, Valentine."

"I'm not the helping sort."

"For money. A good sum of it." He kept his voice low and leaned in closer. "I was robbed, and I need your help to recover what was stolen. I've been told you're an expert in tracking lost items."

My first instinct was to turn and walk away. And by now, I should've learned to trust my instinct, but I didn't. Maybe it was the grief-soaked occasion, or maybe my defenses were down, but I let him continue.

"What was stolen?" I humored him.

"A safe in my apartment was broken into, and they took a laptop computer, along with some money."

"How valuable?"

He paused before answering, his eyes squinting a little as I could see him trying to figure me out. I gave him nothing in return, instead I just waited for an answer.

"It's not about the dollar value," he said. "There's a file on the laptop that's very important to me."

"And you've reported this to the police?"

He hesitated again. It was at that very moment I realized my trust in this guy had hit the floor. Nothing he said felt real. "The Chicago PD investigated the burglary but came up empty-handed. They said that was typical for most situations like this. I didn't give them a full list of everything that was stolen, and I'd prefer to keep the details of the laptop between us. It's not important why it's so valuable to me. But I need it back."

"Fifty-five thousand," I said without hesitation.

"Excuse me?"

"That's my fee," I said. "Take it or leave it."

"And I don't pay a cent if it's not recovered?"

"Five thousand to investigate. Fifty thousand if I recover it." I expected him to negotiate further, to try and show he held the upper hand between us, but to my surprise, he put his hand out, sealing the deal then and there.

As I shook it, I could see Casey walking through the gate, squinting at me.

The look of apprehension on her face said it all—going into business with Mark Costa was a dangerous move.

CHAPTER 2

AFTER CONDUCTING a background check, everything about Mark Costa made me uneasy.

He was paying big money, but no amount of money could make that apprehensive feeling disappear. As I flicked through information on the computer about Mark Costa, the door creaked open. I raised my eyes to see Casey making her way inside, a tray of coffee in one hand. She dropped her bag on the table, lifted one of the take-out cups, and held it out for me.

"Caffeine to start the day, good sir?" she asked, and the moment felt familiar, a sense of déjà vu grabbing me.

"Yes, please."

Casey paused as I took the cup, her smile fading just a little. Not wanting to kill the upbeat mood, I offered a broad smile, but I doubt it made her feel any better. I took a sip, felt the warmth fill my mouth, and then let out an expressive 'ah.'

"That really does hit the spot," I said, lifting the cup up to stare at it. "A day without coffee is like… well, I don't know. I've never had one."

"And if it weren't for coffee, I'm not sure you'd even have a personality. At least not a good one anyway," she said. "What do you call a sad coffee?"

"What?" I squinted.

"A despresso." She laughed hard at the stupidity of her own joke, and I couldn't help but smile with her. Her laughter was infectious, and it broke any tension that remained from the previous night.

Our private investigation firm was on the fifth floor of an office building on Clarke St., in Downtown Chicago. I liked the fifth floor. It stopped the random walk-ins that did nothing but waste our time. Our firm had no signs outside, we didn't advertise, and we had no internet presence. A client would only be able to find our firm if they already knew it existed, but we were never short of work, thanks to word of mouth. Referrals were like gold when it came to our business.

The interior of our office was slick, a professional design, complete with natural light pouring in the tall windows, and filled with modern furniture that looked like it was pulled from the pages of a furniture catalog. I didn't care for the modern scheme, I'd much rather have old furniture and a relaxing atmosphere, but the style suited Casey, and I wasn't going to argue with her about interior design.

"Listen, Jack," her voice softened. "Thank you again for yesterday. The ten-year anniversary was a big one. Just when I thought the memories of Rhys were starting to fade, the memorial reminded me how amazing he was. You would've liked him. He was honorable, like you." She tried to hide her sadness behind a smile, but her eyes told the truth. "And I know it wasn't easy to come to that sort of thing, so, thanks. It meant a lot to me that you were there."

"It was nothing." I took another sip from the cup, hiding behind it. "I was happy to come along and support you."

Silence hung over us for a short moment. Just as I was about to add something about how grief never leaves, and how you grow stronger by the day, the door opened and our first and only client of the day stepped in. Mark Costa stood in the entrance, a blank look on his face. He was dressed in a black suit, fitting snugly on his long, thin torso. His straight black tie exaggerated his slim stomach, and I wondered if he'd ever even had a burger in his life.

"You ready?" His tone was demanding. "Let's get started."

"Good morning, Mark," Casey offered. "Won't you head through to Jack's office?" She pointed to the only other open doorway and waited for our guest to comply.

He paused, looked at my cup, and licked his lips a little. "I'll have a coffee with two sugars."

"We don't serve coffee," I said with a tone devoid of politeness and extended my open palm towards the door. "We have business to discuss."

He looked confused that I'd refused his demand, but he walked into the adjoining room without a complaint. As I followed him, Casey shot me a glance and I fired a wink back at her. This was our castle he'd stepped into, our home, and here, we called the shots.

Casey followed us into the room a few moments later, with her electronic tablet ready to take notes. The separate office was more my style and design. It was darker, with a large oak table in the middle of the room, complete with a number of files and a closed laptop on top, with two chairs in front of the desk, along with my leather chair behind it. There was a bookshelf to the left, exposed brick-work to the right, and a window to the street at the rear, where I usually kept the blinds half-closed.

When we were all seated, I grabbed a notepad from the first drawer of my desk. Writing notes on paper was one of the many qualities that Casey detested about me, but old habits die hard. A good old-fashioned pen and paper was always enough to capture an entire interview, and my messy handwriting was as good as writing in code.

"No notes on the computer," Mark piped up, looking at Casey's tablet. We both looked at him, although I wasn't surprised. "This is strictly off the record. All of it. No bills, no paperwork, and no digital trail. Nothing posted about this anywhere. The risk is too high. I'll pay in cash. This has to be quiet, and there can't be any record that could come back at me later."

Casey hesitated, and then looked at me. When I gave her a brief nod, she placed the tablet down on the desk.

"Ok, Mark," I said. "We're all ears."

For a brief moment, I sensed fear in him. His eyes, the one place no human is capable of hiding the truth, revealed a glimpse of his alarm, but by the time he began speaking, the fear had been masked by an overcoat of arrogance.

"Five days ago, someone stole a number of items from my apartment. They were stored in a safe in my office. Most of the things I can live without, but they stole a laptop that's important to me. The information on it is very valuable." He paused, as if for effect. He sat forward in his chair and drummed his fingers on the edge of my desk in an attempt to amplify his demands. "I need the laptop back. Whatever it takes.

That laptop needs to be back in my hands as soon as possible."

"What's on it?" I asked.

He froze, his eyes lifting to meet mine. "That's irrelevant. The contents of the laptop aren't important. What's important is that the laptop is returned to me. I need to get my hands back on it."

"Whatever is on that laptop is clearly important to you, but if we're going to locate it, we need to know what's on there."

He sat back in his seat as the air in the room began to thicken with tension.

"I'm not about to share the contents—"

"Thank you for coming, Mr. Costa." I stood, cutting off his words mid-sentence, and held my hand out. "But I don't think we're the right private investigators for you. There are others I can recommend, and they'll likely do it for less."

If the moment had been at any other time, it might have been comical, but the look on his face changed in an instant. He raised his eyebrows, staring at me, waiting for me to flinch. I wasn't going to do that. He was hiding something, and whatever it was, it affected him much deeper than any normal stolen item. This item was personal, something that meant the world to him, and when the stakes are that high, it pays to know the full story.

"Alright, alright." He held up his hands in surrender, but refused to give eye contact. "No need to get all upset." He gestured for me to retake my seat, and this time, it was my turn to pause for dramatic effect. It worked and he began to speak again before my butt touched the leather of my chair. "This has to be kept quiet. This information can't get out to the wrong people. The information on that laptop could change a lot of things about my life. I need this investigation to be kept secret, and the information that I'm about to tell you can't leave this room."

"As long as you're paying, then we work for you," Casey said. "We're a professional outfit and know how to manage our client's needs. As long as you keep your end of the bargain, anything discussed between us, stays between us."

He looked out through the window behind me, trying to organize his thoughts. All the focus was on him, and it was clearly how he loved to conduct himself and his business.

"There's evidence on that laptop; evidence of a crime that shall remain unsolved for the time being."

"What kind of evidence?" I asked.

"Does that really matter?"

"It matters. If we're going to work together, then you need to be honest. If the laptop was targeted by someone, then we need to know why." I was growing impatient. "What's the evidence?"

"Ok, look. This isn't easy to share. If this gets out, I'm going to be in some trouble, if you catch my drift."

"It's your choice," I offered, preparing to stand again. He sensed he was walking a tightrope with me, and I was about to cut him loose. "We need the whole truth, or you can walk back out that door."

"It's a video."

"Of?"

"My father."

Those words caught me off-guard. I wasn't expecting that sort of revelation but tried not to show my surprise. "Go on."

"It happened around five years ago, on a night that should've been just like any other. Truth is, that night turned out to be a blessing for me."

"Is it a sex tape of your father?" Casey asked. She was leaning in, a little more intrigued than normal. "Is that what you have on the laptop?"

"I wouldn't dream of ever viewing footage like that of my father," he scoffed, and then pulled his shoulders back. "My father murdered a man, and there's video footage of it."

"Keep talking," I said. He saw me shuffle in my chair and probably figured I'd call it quits right there, but I was intrigued. "Under what circumstances was he murdered?"

"It happened behind Leroy's Bar on Randolph St. Downtown." He drew a breath. "The bar isn't there anymore. It shut down last year after the owner swallowed a bullet. He was shot in a drive-by shooting after closing up one night. It was a random attack, and the police didn't find the shooter. After the shooting, nobody took over the lease. It used to be a popular bar, a local hangout for property developers like my father. He'd finalize a lot of deals in that place."

"I remember the place," I added. "A dive bar full of corrupt businessmen, and dirty deals done dirt cheap."

"That's about right. My father and I had been out for a drink, and we got into an argument with a guy in the bar. He didn't work for us, but he was causing trouble for our property development firm. He left the bar after arguing with us, stumbling all over the place, and Dad suggested that we follow him and talk some sense into him. We followed him outside, and as we exited, we found that he'd decided to relieve himself in the alley. Dad followed him into the alley, threatened him, and then the guy pulled a gun. My father wrestled with him, and the gun went off. It was self-defense. He died right there on the spot and..." He paused again. "And that was that."

"I assume the cops weren't called in on this?"

"They were called later. I remember hearing about his death on the news, but we left no evidence of our involvement. We had to get rid of it all. We couldn't risk it. After Dad shot the man, I looked around and saw there were no witnesses, so we were safe, but then I noticed that Leroy's had one camera above the back door that was pointed straight at us. The camera was there to keep the staff safe when using the back entrance to throw the trash in the dumpsters. Dad took the guy's gun, and I went back into Leroy's and offered the owner $5,000 for the video, no questions asked. He said $25,000 in cash and I agreed, right there on the spot. He said the feed from the video went straight into a laptop, and it wasn't stored anywhere else. He knew I was good for the cash, so I took the laptop and told him I'd deliver the cash the next day. After I had the laptop, we walked away. We left the body where it had fallen and got out of there. I was sure nobody had seen us, and we were carrying any evidence of what happened that night. My father told me to destroy the laptop and he'd get rid of the gun."

"Did you pay the owner the money?" I questioned. "Yes."

"And the cops never came and questioned you?" Casey asked. "You were never suspects in the crime?"

21

"Never."

I leaned forward, resting my elbows on the table. "But you didn't make the laptop disappear, did you?"

"You're clever, Jack." He smirked, an expression that felt as honest as his deception. "No, I didn't destroy the laptop. I kept it for a while, and once I knew the time was right, I did what needed to be done."

"It was blackmail," Casey said. "You used that footage against your father."

"I call it taking control of the business." He didn't even blink at the revelation. "I used the evidence to my advantage. It was good business sense. My father was running the firm into the ground, turning soft in his old age and costing me money; money that I had every right to protect. He might've built the firm from nothing, but he'd lost his business skills over the years before that. He got comfortable, looking after his friends, rather than focusing on the bottom line of the business. So I told him that I would take over the business, and if he argued about it, then the footage would fall into the wrong hands. He tried to fight me on it, but I held firm. Within five days of revealing I had kept the laptop, I was in complete control of the firm, and he was out the door. It had to be done to save the business."

"Whatever helps you sleep at night," I said. "So you kept the laptop all this time?"

"It was an insurance policy against my father if he ever thought about making a move to take over the company again," Mark crossed one leg over the other. Despite revealing that he was an accomplice to murder, he appeared comfortable. "Now that you know the story, I don't think I need to emphasize the importance of that laptop. I need it back."

"So you can continue to blackmail your father?" Casey questioned.

"So I can continue to run a company that employs hundreds of loyal employees. People that have devoted a lot of time to the business. People with families. Without my guidance, those employees don't have a job, they don't get paid, and they don't get to put food on the table for their families. If it wasn't for people like me, the city would fall apart. I'm the hero here. I'm—"

"Your father is suspect number one," Casey cut him off before he could continue to build up his ego. "If that's what you used to blackmail—sorry, negotiate—then he could've tried to get it back."

"I don't think it was him. He couldn't get access to my apartment."

"Maybe he hired someone to get it. A professional thief?"

"If he'd taken the laptop, I would've heard about it the second it was in his hands. He would've tried to take back the business. His name is still on the business papers, because I haven't been able to remove him yet." He shook his head. "No. Whoever took it is holding it for another reason."

"Do you have an idea who that would be?"

"If I did, we wouldn't be sitting here." He grunted. "The security footage went haywire that week, which I don't think is a coincidence, and there's no footage of the foyer or the hallway that leads to my apartment. Everyone that I thought could be a suspect has been cleared by the police. They all have alibis. That's why I'm here."

"I'm sure we'll find a lead soon enough," I paused,

tapping my finger on the edge of the desk, and then asked the most obvious question of all. "Who has access to your apartment?"

"I live alone. It's just me and the personal friends that I bring home." He leaned his head back. "Other than the security guards, it's just me."

"I assume you have a cleaner?" Casey asked.

"She cleans twice times a week, but she doesn't have keys. The security guards let her in."

I leaned forward and studied him. "You're asking us to find a laptop that holds evidence of an unsolved crime."

"I'm paying you fifty-five thousand to find a laptop that I bought for twenty-five thousand dollars." Arrogance was part of his DNA, a part of his soul. It was an unshakable feature of his demeanor, as clear as his Italian heritage. "That laptop is mine and it was stolen from me. That's illegal."

I looked at Casey, and when she nodded to confirm her approval of the job, I turned back to Mark. "We'll take the job."

"What are you going to do first?" He questioned, uncomfortable under my stare. "Where are you going to start?"

I waited for a few moments, and then leaned back in the chair. "Let's get one thing clear first—you need to give us space. We need time to work. If we need your help, we'll ask for it, otherwise we expect to be left alone." I waited for him to respond to the demand, and when he nodded his approval, I continued. "For the investigation, we need a copy of the police report, we need to look at the room it was stolen from, we need to search your apartment, and we need your ideas on who you think stole it. I also need notes on anyone you've had conflict with over the last year. I need all that information as soon as possible."

"I'll get my assistant to drop off those notes within the hour," he nodded and took an envelope from his coat pocket. He placed it on the table. "I'll be at my apartment at 5pm tonight. You can come and look at the room then."

I stood again, reached out, and checked the envelope. It felt like five-thousand in cash. I wasn't going to count it in front of him, although I would count it later. I didn't trust this man at all. If he could swindle a child out of five dollars, I'm sure he would.

Mark also rose from his chair. "Are we good?"

"50k if we find it and return it to you," I said. "If that's the agreement, then we're good."

"Done." He turned to walk out of the office, but before he got to the door, he turned and looked back at us. "Just keep it quiet. My father is," he shrugged, "not a very nice man."

I nodded and he walked out the door. When we were alone, I looked at Casey, and she looked at me. No more words were needed.

We'd stepped into danger, stepped into the seedy underworld of corrupt property developments, and I was sure there'd be trouble ahead.

CHAPTER 3

IT ALWAYS amazed me how some families operated, and from what I could tell about the Costas, they were a family I wanted no part of. Blackmail. Murder. Corruption. From a quick search of the internet, crime appeared to be part of their family's DNA. The hateful disgust Mark had for his father was clear, and I was sure the shooting of a man in an alley five years ago wasn't the only murder in their family's past.

Within two hours of our first meeting, Mark's personal assistant had dropped off a number of files, including the police report, a list of the people he suspected, and a copy of his work diary. While we waited, we'd conducted our own preliminary investigations. Mark was divorced with two kids, who currently lived in New York and only saw their father once a year. He owned two businesses, recently purchased an apartment in an upscale building, and owned a Porsche and a Bentley. Very little presence on social media, however, his face had been splashed around the social pages of Chicago for various functions. He was a high-flyer. A mover and shaker. A player. An assassin behind a fake smile.

He'd had photos taken with politicians, sports stars, and movie icons, and his confidence and arrogance almost jumped out of every photo. But behind the fake smile and sleazy grin, there was a long line of people who he'd had conflicts with. He'd been accused of punching another developer. He was seen shouting at his staff almost daily. And he was rumored to be physically abusive towards his ex-wife. Wherever he went, Mark seemed to have left a trail of issues behind.

"He's always been slippery," Casey said as she read over the police report of the robbery. "That's nothing new."

"What do you know about him personally?" I returned. I still wasn't sure why I'd accepted the job. There was something about him that just didn't sit right, and one look at Casey only seemed to further my suspicions.

"Shrewd businessman in a world of shrewd businessmen. I say shrewd, but I really mean corrupt. Lots of dodgy deals and lots of off-the-book payments. The whole world that he's involved in is corrupt. If we go down this path, then we're getting a behind-the-scenes look into the world of dishonest property developers." She shook her head at the thought. "Mark played baseball with Rhys, and when he couldn't make it big, he turned to his family business, which was property development. He runs Costa and Trust developments, which has a reputation for developments that are built quickly. They're known for cutting corners. His father—"

"Sergio Costa," I grunted.

"You know him?"

"Sergio and I have a little history. I doubt he would remember." I nodded, remembering why I knew the family name. "It was a case I had ten years ago that involved one of Sergio's business associates, a typical piece of gutter trash, a man who was unfaithful to his wife. The wife had hired me to find evidence of the affair, and then present it to the cheater. I confronted the man at a worksite with photos of him and his mistress, and Sergio came in to defend his friend with all guns blazing. I pushed Sergio Costa away, and he fell over. Later that night, five thugs were waiting outside my apartment. It wasn't a pretty ending—not for me or the thugs."

"Sounds like an average night for you," Casey said. "I didn't have a lot to do with Mark, but he and Rhys were friends. They were on the same baseball team for years. Mostly, I remember that I never trusted him. There was always something about Mark that seemed off. Rhys was such a great guy—he was always looking after others who were rejected by the popular groups. Rhys was always helping the people who others ignored, and I guess he didn't want anyone to feel forgotten, like the way he felt growing up. That's why he went out of his way to be friendly to Mark."

She paused, looking into the distance and hanging onto the moment. I could already see that this wasn't going to be easy for her. Mark Costa was just a little too close to the same grief she'd experienced the previous day. The next few days would test her resilience, of that, I was sure.

"I still miss Rhys, you know," she said, staring absently out through the window. "Rhys was an unlucky kid who had a great break. Growing up in foster homes, we'd ended up in the same place a number of times. He was like a brother to me. Not 'like' a brother, he was a brother. Not blood, but he was the family I chose. We both knew the pain of not knowing our parents, we both knew the pain of never quite belonging somewhere in our childhood. Sports was the escape for Rhys. That was his way of belonging somewhere and that drove him to be so good at baseball. Rhys would've made it to the big time. I had no doubt about it. We stayed close over the years, and he always had my back. When I was having trouble when I was fifteen, he was the first one there. He would've flown to the other side of the world to help me out." She sighed and then drew a long breath. "Some days are a lot harder than others. Time seems to go by so fast, but when I think of Rhys, sometimes it feels like a hundred years have passed, but at the same time, like it's only been a day."

"Grief is the price we pay for love."

"So true. It reminds me of a baseball card I gave Rhys on the night he was killed. It was a 1992 Turk Wendell card; the picture was of the player brushing his teeth between innings. The card was so memorable because this player had all sorts of superstitions, including brushing his teeth between each inning, so that was the picture they put on the baseball card. Not a picture of him pitching, or catching, or training, but of him brushing his teeth in his Cubs uniform. Turk Wendell was his idol, the person he wanted to be. He loved that card so much, laughing each time he'd spotted it. A week before Rhys died, he was on the verge of becoming the starter in the Minor League team, so I thought I'd get the card to congratulate him. I searched for it, placed a bid, and won the card. I had it all packaged up in an envelope, along with a note. I gave it to him the night he died, and he was so happy. He laughed so much. I'm happy that was our last memory together. Like a lot of people who lose loved ones suddenly, I didn't get the chance to say goodbye, but he knew I loved him. I was lucky I could give it to him before he died."

"If you remember him, then he's still alive, at least in here." I tapped my hand on my heart. "And I know the player. Turk Wendell had a few baseball cards like that—one of him jumping over the baseline, and another of him eating licorice. You were a good little sister to seek it out for him."

I could see she was close to tears and wondered whether I'd made a mistake taking the case in the first place. Perhaps I should've been more mindful. Casey moved to the other side of the room and wheeled out the whiteboard from the meeting room. I stayed seated behind my desk, knowing better than to disturb her when she was focused.

"Suspects," she wiped her eyes with the back of her sleeve and then held the pen ready to write a list on the whiteboard. "List them off."

"Mark," I fired.

"You think he's lying?" Casey asked.

"There's missing a laptop. I believe that. Was it stolen?" I shrugged. "I don't know. He could be asking us to find a laptop that wasn't even his in the first place. Or he could be asking us to find someone else's laptop. I don't trust a word that man said, and he could be lying to us about ever owning the laptop."

"Interesting." She wrote his name on the board. "Next?"

"Sergio Costa."

"The father, of course. Sounds to me like he'd be the prime candidate. If the burglary really happened, then he's got to be the number one suspect. His motive is clear as he's got the most to gain by getting his hands on that laptop." Casey wrote the name on the board and then paused. "Just imagine that. Imagine being blackmailed by your own child into giving up your life's work. That would've hurt."

"Don't forget that Sergio killed a man and never reported it. It's hard to feel anything for someone willing to commit murder and leave the body for the rats. And I'm sure it's not the only murder he's been involved in, because his name used to be feared. I used to hear his name a lot, and I often wondered what happened to him, but I figured he'd been knocked off like every other influential crook."

"Right," Casey agreed. "Next?"

"The other people with access to the apartment. The security guards and the cleaner."

"Access to the apartment and enough time to set it up. They could've targeted the apartment for the cash, and the laptop was a bonus. When they saw it was worthless, they might've thrown it out. No other motive for the laptop as yet." Casey made more notes on the whiteboard. "Any more?"

"Julian Wright, another property developer, is at the top of the list of people Costa has had conflicts with. He's noted that they've had a few fights over numerous development contracts." I read the names that Mark had put together for us. "And a person named Jim Tanner, yet another property developer, known for having connections to the mob."

"Julian Wright and Jim Tanner," Casey continued to write on the board. "Any more?"

"Those are our top five and the place we'll have to start. More will follow, but this is the beginning of the investigation," I said. "Right now, we need more information about Mark Costa. Did he have other enemies that were hunting him down? Did he have other people who hated him? Has he done any big deals lately? And was it common knowledge he was blackmailing his father?"

"I'll talk with some of Mark's friends, those that knew Rhys as well. I know he keeps in contact with a few of them, for business purposes." Casey stood back and looked at the names on the board. "I'll have a way to talk to them if I mention Rhys."

"Perfect," I said. "People like Mark Costa are driven by the need for success, attention, power. He's chasing his place in this world, chasing validation, because he never found it at home. We know he'll step on his own family to get what he wants."

"I just can't believe he'd use that video footage to blackmail him. I mean, his own father," she repeated. It wasn't unusual for honest people to struggle with the ways of the dishonest. "Not that I know what having a father means. I've never met mine, and I guess if I met my father, I wouldn't hesitate to blackmail him. But first, I'd punch him in the nose for leaving my sister and me to grow up in foster homes."

I didn't respond. Not because I didn't want to, I cared deeply about Casey, but because I didn't know what to say. My family wasn't perfect, but I knew their faults. Casey never had the privilege of even discovering their faults for herself.

"Sorry," she said. "It gets under my skin sometimes. People like Mark have everything handed to them, never have to struggle for a dime, and they still treat people terribly. I don't get that."

Our private investigation business meant we had

access to a vast range of people, those from all walks of life. It didn't matter whether they were upper class, middle class, or working class—people had a way of stooping to the lowest levels of humanity in order to get what they wanted. After decades in the business, few things shocked me, and this case was just like so many others I had worked before. And it would also not be the last.

"If you ever want to talk about your family—"

"Talk to you?" Casey laughed. "Are you serious? I'd get more of a reaction out of a brick wall than you, Jack. Emotions aren't exactly your strong suit."

"I was going to suggest that I'd pay for someone for you to talk to," I smiled. "You know, the only time I went to a psychologist, she said I should write letters to the people I hate, and later on, I should burn them. I did that, but then I didn't know what to do with all the letters I wrote."

"See?" She laughed. "Anytime emotions become too much for you, you joke about it and laugh it off. You'd make a terrible psychologist."

"But at least I make a decent investigator," I laughed.

I stood and walked to the window, gazing across the skyline as my mind wandered about the intricacies of the meeting. There was a lot more to this case than Mark Costa was willing to admit, and I needed to be sure I wasn't aiding and abetting a crime, regardless of how long ago the murder took place. There was no statute of limitations on murder, and I didn't need to become an accessory after the fact. There'd been times in my past where I took risks for clients, but this was not going to be one of them. Mark Costa was not the kind of man who I'd risk my career for. Not today, and not ever.

"There'll be questions asked once we find this laptop." I took a deep breath. "And we might have to find the answers."

I heard Casey stand and take a few steps to stand next to me by the window. She stood in silence and appreciated the beautiful day, the sun glistening off the tops of passing vehicles. Despite the start of summer being within striking distance, there was a possible snowstorm predicted.

"If we find that laptop, there'll be many more questions," she agreed. "Where will you begin?"

I thought for a moment, although not about the case's suspects. It was more to do with the murder of the mystery man, gunned down in an alley long ago and left to die. I wondered where that case stood today and whether the police report sat in some long-forgotten computer file, or perhaps the file even lived on a physical shelf amongst other cold cases.

The victim's family haunted me the most, because I could only imagine the pain and grief they would've endured during the years since that fateful night. Years with no answers and no end to their pain, left to deal with not only the grief, but the lack of justice as well. Another unsolved murder in Chicago, where almost fifty percent of murders went unsolved, year in, year out.

"Jack?"

I turned, and Casey could see where my mind was at, although she didn't say. Perhaps she'd had the same thoughts.

"Can you search for any unsolved murders around Leroy's Bar at that time? Let's find out who the murdered guy is. It might be a lead. The family of the murdered man may know about the laptop."

"There's a list of cold cases on the CPD website. I'll look into any murders around Randolph St. from five years ago." Casey made a note on her pad. "What about you?"

I looked at my watch. After a day of preliminary investigations, it was already the afternoon. "First, we need to go and look at the apartment. That's going to tell us a lot. After that, I'll try to chat with Sergio Costa. I'll have to approach him cautiously because I remember him as a corrupt, ruthless, and dangerous man," I walked to the coat rack and grabbed my leather jacket. "And that's just the nice things I have to say about him."

CHAPTER 4

THE FOYER to Five-Pillar Residences, on one of Downtown Chicago's most expensive streets, Michigan Ave., was glitzy, glamorous, and extravagant. The former headquarters of a failed bank, the towers had been redeveloped in 2015 into residences for the ultra-rich. I was in awe as I stepped through the doors to the foyer. The soaring ceiling heights, the intricate tracery, and the lavish terraces were spectacular, and along with the exceptional architectural details, it took my breath away.

Mark Costa was waiting for us in the foyer, talking on the phone, sitting on one of the artfully arranged lounge seats. Costa stood when he saw us, and then held out his hand as a stop sign while he finished the call. His arrogance was almost unbearable, and it took all my self-control not to reach out and break at least one of his soft fingers. Casey sensed this and rested her hand on my elbow and mouthed the words, 'stay calm.'

Costa finished the call and didn't welcome us or offer his hand for us to shake. He looked at his watch instead. "You're on time. That's good."

I drew a breath and looked at the doorman. "Has he got access to your place?"

"Him? No." Costa shook his head. "He's not security. I'll introduce you to the security guards once we're down in the parking lot. They have an office down there." He looked across the foyer and saw a man enter the side door to the foyer and pointed at him. "That's Ivan Pushkin. He's the head of security."

Ivan stopped and looked over at us. He was a tall man, broad-shouldered, with a solid chest. He looked like he hadn't expressed any emotion in years, and like his Russian-sounding name, his haircut made him look like he was straight out of the former Soviet Union. Dressed in a black suit, he looked professional, and it seemed to be the uniform of choice for the staff in the building.

"These are the two investigators I told you about," Costa called out and waved him over. "They want to talk to you about the break-in and why your stupid cameras didn't capture who broke into my apartment."

Ivan walked across the foyer to us, stared at Costa for a long moment, as if trying to resist the urge to punch him in the mouth as well, and then nodded. "I'll be in my office when you're ready." His accent was thick Russian. "I'll be waiting."

He turned and walked towards the service elevator.

"I don't know what those lazy pricks do all day." Costa looked over his shoulder at the service elevator at the far side of the room. Ivan entered the elevator without turning around. "What are you looking for in my apartment?"

"Any evidence that the cops missed," I said. "Even the smallest thing that they might have missed could help us. And we'll also do a sweep for bugs."

"Bugs?" Costa scoffed. "This isn't a James Bond movie."

"They're more common than you imagine," Casey

said. "And they come in all different sizes and disguises. There are devices you can get on eBay very cheaply—there's even one that looks and functions just like a USB charging cable. If you're not looking for it, you'll think it's just a benign charging cable, but what you don't realize is that it's got a mobile phone SIM card in it. You can buy devices for less than $50. You can get devices that look like outlets, smoke detectors, or light fixtures. It wouldn't surprise me if you have one in there."

"So you'll sweep the place?" Mark seemed angry that we were about to enter into his personal space. "The whole apartment?"

"We will." I tapped the bag I was carrying as the service elevator pinged again. "We'll check everything."

Costa looked across the foyer to the elevator, and out stepped a woman who looked in her mid-thirties, dressed in a blue uniform. The woman headed for the side exit, but Costa called out after her. "Lauren."

The brunette woman stopped and turned around. Costa led us towards her.

"This is Lauren Taylor, my cleaner." Costa pointed at her like she was a second-rate citizen, although I was sure that's how he treated most people. "She's here twice a week to make my apartment spotless. She does an adequate job."

"Hello, Lauren," Casey offered her hand as a sign of respect. Lauren shook it gently. "My name is Casey May, and this is Jack Valentine. We're investigating the recent robbery in Mr. Costa's apartment. Do you have a moment to talk?"

"Don't worry about that now," Costa was dismissive of her and turned back to Casey. "You can talk with Lauren later and find out what she saw." He looked at his watch. "You've got thirty minutes to search my apartment. I'm not going to wait around forever."

"Access card." I stuck out my hand to Costa. If he was going to treat others terribly, I was going to do the same to him.

When I talked to his assistant earlier, I gave her clear instructions that Costa couldn't be in the apartment while we were searching it. I needed the freedom to think and to wander around the apartment without the pressure of someone looking over my shoulder. If there was a clue in there, it'd be hidden away, and we wouldn't find it if Mark was telling us what we could and couldn't touch.

Costa squinted, drew a breath, and then reached into his pocket and handed me the access card. Casey took down Lauren's details, thanked her, and then turned back to Costa. "We'll meet you in the parking lot in forty-five minutes."

Costa looked at his watch again, resisting the urge to argue about the time we needed, and then stormed out the front doors, phone in hand, ready to yell at someone else.

Casey turned back to Lauren, who was still standing next to us. "Sorry about him."

"Don't worry about it." Lauren's voice was soft. "It's his usual behavior. I'm used to it."

Casey raised her eyebrows at me as Lauren walked away. We headed towards the residents' elevator, swiped the access card, and Casey hit the button for the twenty-fifth floor. The doors closed with a faint swish, and once we were off, soft elevator music began to emanate from somewhere above. It only added to the luxurious ambiance. Light suddenly spilled into our mode of transport as we left the confines of the foyer and continued to climb along the outside of the building. Soon, the skyscrapers were visible in the distance, each glistening in the evening sunset.

I watched the numbers climbing on the display above us. The elevator began to slow down, and we waited for the doors to open again once the familiar ping of hitting the requested floor echoed above the previously tranquil soundtrack. A wide hallway opened before us, giving us the impression of a five-star hotel. Everything was a brilliant white, right down to the handle on the two doors on opposite sides of the hall.

"Was he involved in this redevelopment?" Casey asked as we walked towards the entrance to his apartment.

"Luckily, no," I held the card over the scanner next to the entrance, and when the light went green, I opened the door. "The Costas mostly build commercial developments and had no hand in the redesign of this place."

My mouth fell open as I stepped into Costa's apartment. The place had a view that tourists would pay top dollar for. It was appointed with the most luxurious finishes: custom millwork and cabinetry, top-dollar appliances, and wide plank white oak wood floors. It was everything capitalist dreams are made of. But while it was awe-inspiring, I couldn't help thinking it was the validation Costa needed to prove to himself that he was successful.

The vast expanse of the apartment only became really apparent once we stepped down a small flight of stairs from the front door. It opened up into a huge space, with another staircase on the opposite wall going up towards the sleeping areas of the apartment. A massive wall of sheer glass stretched the length of one side, with dual sliding doors currently open to allow the fresh air inside. The outdoor area had two sun lounges, plus an outdoor table with seating for ten. An outdoor spa topped off the impressive balcony.

There were a number of objects a thief would steal right from this room, and my first thoughts were about why they hadn't. After the initial shock about the size of the apartment subsided, Casey headed for the stairs, and I followed. Whatever we needed to see was located in the home office and it was the logical place to start.

I stopped at the top of the stairs and turned once more to look across the living space. There was a camera mounted in one corner, and from where it was located, it had a complete view of the room we stood in, as well as a decent portion of the outside area. A tiny red light on its base gave the impression that it was hard at work.

The corridor leading to the office was wide and brightly lit. Four open doors revealed a huge main bathroom, a second bedroom, and one room that looked more like an office area, with several rows of boxes stacked three high. This was clearly where the laptop was stolen from.

I entered the room, noting every detail—a desk against the far wall, a cupboard to the side of the room, an armchair in the back corner. I could see that the safe, normally hidden behind the desk, sat open and empty like a disgraced soldier that had fallen asleep on duty. The safe's locking mechanism was a simple keypad, and the digital readout displayed five bright red zeroes. I shut it, punched in five zeroes, and it opened again. I groaned. What was the use of having a safe if the code could be guessed in one try?

Whilst we searched the room, it was Casey that first aired what had been crossing my mind since the moment we'd arrived. "We won't find much evidence in here," she said. "It looks like everything has been sprayed with disinfectant, then scrubbed, and then hit with a power hose."

"This place looks more sterile than a hospital," I agreed. "How could anyone be comfortable in a place like this?"

After another five minutes of searching the room, I opened my kit bag, and grabbed the scanner. The listening devices could've been hidden anywhere— behind paintings on office walls, in ceilings and desk drawers, in light fixtures, and even wired into the doorframe. The scanner reacted as I moved it over the desk in the corner of the room.

"We've got one," I said to Casey, reaching inside the lamp on the desk. I removed a small item that looked like a watch battery. "That means this was definitely a planned robbery."

"If it was planted for that purpose," Casey scanned her eyes over the bug. "A man like Costa, well, he could have people tracking him for all sorts of different reasons."

We both nodded. That was a very real possibility.

"Initial thoughts?" I asked her as I popped open the bug, deactivating it.

"This looks like an inside job," she said. "Or at least it was done with help from the inside."

"You read my mind. There's a security system both inside this apartment as well as outside," I said, pointing to another camera in this room, "This is a building with working cameras and active security personnel. It must've been someone pretty well-known to be able to gain entry. The person could've paid someone to sneak around."

"The guard seemed nervous, but he could've been nervous about losing his job," Casey said. "His job is to protect the apartments, and he wasn't able to do that."

As she finished the sentence, something caught Casey's eye. She walked over to the corner of the room, leaned down, and reached behind the desk. She pulled an item out and held it up for me to see—a bracelet dangling back and forth between her fingers.

"To M. With Love, Mark," Casey read as she tilted her head a little sideways. "First question—who's M? And second question—why is it in this room?"

I walked over and Casey dropped the piece of jewelry into my open palm. It felt heavy, which also made it expensive. One thing I knew about gold jewelry was that the purchaser paid based on its weight, and this felt like a few thousand dollars at least.

"Think someone dropped it?" I looked around the room again. "Or perhaps Costa hadn't given it to the recipient yet?"

Casey nodded, then followed me back out into the corridor. We spent the next twenty-five minutes searching the rest of the apartment, scanning a separate room each, until we met at the main bedroom. There was no door at the end of the corridor, with the master bedroom opening up before us. It had a sunken floor, with a huge king-sized bed against one wall, and another impressive wall of glass in front of it. There wasn't much to find in the room, and as appealing as it was, we soon returned to the main living area.

"Well, Mr. Valentine?" Casey said. "When are you going to give me the pay raise that will afford me something like this?"

I laughed, watching as she took a final stroll down the stairs and out onto the outdoor balcony. I followed and instantly regretted it, feeling a burst of jealousy directed at the man who actually did call this place home. I looked at my watch, and we'd already spent fifty-five minutes in the apartment. I was surprised Costa hadn't called us out yet.

"Let's get out of here. We're not going to find much more," I muttered and turned towards the door. Casey stalled for a moment longer, taking in the view, then followed me out, shaking her head the entire time.

"Did you notice that he didn't have one photo of his kids?" Casey commented as we entered the elevator to ride down to the parking garage. "Not exactly Dad-of-the-year material."

"I noticed," I said. "What I also noticed was that this place is layered in security. There's no way anyone could've gotten in there without help. Perhaps this mystery woman 'M' could help us."

We pondered that thought for a few moments, and when we arrived in the parking garage, Costa was waiting by one of his cars, staring at his phone.

"Good," he said once he saw us exit the elevator. "What did you find?"

"A bug," I replied. "I need to see your car."

"What?" His mouth dropped open. "Like a listening bug? Where?"

"In the room the laptop was stolen from, under the lamp on the desk." I held out the bug and gave it to him. He stared at it, confused.

"Someone placed this inside my apartment? What for?"

"That's what we need to find out," Casey said. "If our suspicions are correct, then they'll have placed trackers on your cars as well."

Costa shook his head in disbelief but pointed towards his two cars. "These are my cars—a Porsche and the more practical Bentley. I use the sports car around the city and the Bentley for longer drives."

I pointed Casey to the Bentley, and I headed towards the Porsche. Costa unlocked both cars, and we went to work. I ran my hands under the seats and inside the door. Nothing. I moved to the trunk, and there was nothing of interest. Lying down on the ground and looking under the vehicle, it didn't take me long to find what I was looking for. It was tucked near the back tire, taped onto the car's body with black electrical tape. I reached my arm under the low-lying Porsche, removed the device, and then stood, waving it in the air for Costa to see.

"An old iPhone?" he asked. "Whose is that?"

"That's a good question," I responded. I unlocked it without a passcode, and there was only one app on the screen— 'Track my phone.'

"What does that mean?" Costa looked over my shoulder. "Someone was listening to my conversations when I was in my car?"

"Not listening—tracking. This phone was plugged into this charger," I reached back under the car and picked it up. "And then the charger was connected to the mains of the vehicle. Any time the car was running, the battery was charging. They stuck it on there with black electrical tape. Easy enough to do from watching a couple of videos on the internet. It takes about five minutes to set up. Anybody could've set this up anywhere at any time. All they'd need is five minutes."

"I don't understand?" Mark squinted as he looked at the phone.

"They were using the phone to track your whereabouts. They knew when you'd left the building, they knew where you parked the car, and they knew when you were coming back. It's a very cheap, but very effective, tracking device."

Casey came over to us, holding another cell phone in the air. "You too?"

"That's right," I responded. "Whoever stole that laptop knew you weren't home."

Whether it was an inside job didn't matter. What we knew was that we were dealing with someone who targeted the laptop.

And that meant we were dealing with someone who knew about its contents.

CHAPTER 5

COSTA RAPPED his knuckles on the white wooden door that led to the security office, and it wasn't long before Ivan Pushkin opened it. He didn't smile or greet us. He stood still without expressing emotion, not even acknowledging our presence with the slightest of smiles or nods. His hand rested on the door. He was clean-shaven. Well-groomed. His suit was clean and tidy. We waited for him to greet us, but he simply stood there, tall and strong, waiting to be spoken to.

"They'd like to ask you a few questions, Ivan." Costa was at his condescending worse. "That's if you've got the time, although I couldn't imagine that you'd be busy doing anything else. You're certainly not protecting this building."

Ivan stared at him with his cold eyes. Costa was over six feet tall, but Ivan still towered over him. He would tower over most people, even standing a little taller than me at six-foot-four. The security guard stepped back from the door, leaving it open, and returned to his chair. I stepped in the doorway and glanced around the room. The security office was a roomy space, well-lit by a number of ceiling lights. There was a table in the middle of the room, a whiteboard to the left, and five monitors on the back wall. They flicked between camera feeds on a rotational basis, scanning the foyer, hallways, elevators, and gym. The air smelled like a strong air freshener, and I couldn't spot a speck of dust.

"Can they be trusted?" Ivan sat down, typed two lines into his computer, and then swiveled his chair to stare at me. "He doesn't look trustworthy."

"Maybe I should ask the same question of you," I stepped closer to him. "Because, right now, you're suspect number one for this robbery. This job had to have inside help, and you're the man with the most knowledge of the systems here."

He didn't flinch. He kept his cold eyes on mine.

"We'd like to ask you some simple questions," Casey softened her voice. Her feminine touch was required to ease the tension. "Nothing too complicated."

Ivan broke from my stare and looked at Casey. She smiled broadly, and he nodded.

"Do you work the night shift?" Casey closed the door behind her.

"No." His answer was blunt. He didn't continue.

"But you work the day shift and manage the office?" I asked.

"Yes."

"That's not exactly helpful, Ivan," Costa said, leaning against the back wall, hands in his pockets. "Here, in this country, we provide more than one-word answers. If you had an American education, you'd understand that."

Ivan slowly turned around to face Costa. I had to agree with Ivan on this one—it was hard not to punch Costa in the face when he was at his arrogant worst.

"We'd like access to the video footage for the week before the burglary took place, please. We'd also like to see if there has been any unauthorized access to the parking lot in the week before," Casey used her soft tone again. "It would help us a lot in the investigation about the burglary, which I'm sure you're as anxious as we are to solve."

"Of course." Ivan drew a breath and then turned to Casey. "I will help you and give you the files. The day before the burglary, we had a scheduled upgrade to the video recording systems which caused issues during a five-hour period. This scheduled upgrade had been planned for five weeks. Notifications were limited to internal staff and residents that the systems were being upgraded."

"And it's during the upgrade that the burglary took place," Costa added. "Can't trust these guys to do anything right. I pay top-dollar for this place and its security, and I get people like him."

"We informed the residents that this was happening, and we doubled our security staff on the doors," Ivan added. "We were monitoring the situation."

"Not well enough," Costa added. "My apartment still got broken into, remember?"

"Ok," Casey held out her open palm to calm Costa down. "If we could have a look at the video files, that would be very helpful."

"I'll transfer them to a USB drive for you," he said. "It will be ready tomorrow."

"We've read the statement that you gave to the police, but is there anything else you can remember about that night?" Casey continued. "Was there anything at all that could be helpful?"

"No." Again, his answer was blunt.

It was clear we weren't going to get anything out of him while Costa was nearby. Casey looked at me, and I nodded.

"Thank you for your help, Ivan," Casey said. "I'll be back tomorrow morning to pick up that USB drive."

Ivan didn't respond as we walked out the door.

"Real helpful, eh?" Costa said as he stepped out of the office and shut the door behind him. "Useless security guards. If they worked for me, I'd fire them all."

The three of us walked in silence through the parking lot to the elevator. The elevator arrived quickly after Costa pushed the button, and when the doors closed after we were inside, I turned to Costa.

"Who's M?" I said.

"'M'?"

"We found a bracelet in the office, behind the desk, that said, 'To M, With Love, Mark.'"

He drew a breath and ran his fingers through his hair. "That was… it was for my ex-wife, but there was an error with the engraving. It must've fallen down behind the desk."

I didn't respond, mostly because I didn't believe him. He was lying, and I wasn't sure why.

"So, have you solved it yet?" Costa asked when the elevator doors opened to the foyer. "Do you know where to find the laptop? Because I need it back, and I need it back now."

"We know where to begin," I replied. "And we'll keep you updated on our progress."

I turned and walked through the foyer, Casey by my side. We were silent until we reached my truck, parked a block down from the apartment building.

"Getting information from that security guard was like getting blood from a stone," I said as I fired up the truck. "He wasn't giving us much."

"It's his culture. He doesn't respond well to intimidation," Casey said. "He looks Russian."

"I tell you what—he wasn't 'Russian' to help us."

"That's a terrible Dad joke," Casey smiled and opened her phone. She made a number of notes before she turned to me. "Do you think Ivan Pushkin could've done it?"

"Not by himself." I pulled out into the rush-hour traffic and started the drive back to our office. "If he's involved, he was working for someone else."

"An inside man that knew exactly when the security cameras were going to be out and knew where the security guards were going to be monitoring," Casey agreed. "Where to next?"

"I need you to investigate our security guard's past, see if there's anything unusual, any connections to the other suspects, or if he's got a criminal record. Have it ready for tomorrow morning," I said. "And I'm going to talk to the person most likely to have employed him."

CHAPTER 6

IT DIDN'T take long to find Sergio Costa's whereabouts, the once-ruthless property developer cast aside by an equally ruthless successor to his throne. After a quick Google search, I found that Sergio had purchased a small restaurant in Northbrook, a small suburb on the northern edge of Cook County. It surprised me that a man like Sergio Costa was still alive. Most people in the criminal world met their end long before they made it to retirement age.

As the traffic on the Interstate took on its usual stop-start monotony, I thumbed the radio on. I didn't mind that the drive would be around thirty-five minutes. My truck was a place to think, a place where my mind was free to wander, a place where case after case had been solved. But instead of work, my thoughts turned to my wife Claire as I shuffled my way through the evening traffic. Beautiful, sweet Claire, the savior to so many, a hero to the children she taught. And to me, she was so, so much more. Man, how I missed her.

Someone behind me honked, and I looked up to see that I'd slowed down. Claire had always had that kind of effect on me, the kind that would capture my every attention, with the rest of the world fading away whenever she was near. The honk changed my mood in an instant, the anger and pain of losing her still raw in my mind. I accepted long ago that it would always be raw. Losing my wife in a mass shooting was always going to be an open wound, an emotional hole that I could never fix.

The radio provided a distraction, with Freddy Mercury launching into Bohemian Rhapsody as I kept the tempo with my fingers drumming on the steering wheel. It was a much better way of beating the traffic blues, and when Billy Joel took over from Freddy, my focus on the job had returned.

I parked across the street from Sergio Costa's restaurant and sat for a few minutes to take inventory of the surroundings. I didn't know a lot about Northbrook, apart from it's high school served as the filming location for the 1980s teenage classic film, The Breakfast Club. From my first glance of the streets, the suburb appeared full of money, comfort, and security. Older people walked the sidewalks, families rode past on bicycles, and there didn't seem to be a bit of graffiti anywhere. Not the sort of place I expected to find a former crime boss.

From the outside, Sergio Costa's restaurant looked like any other standard eating establishment. The name, 'Apex,' loomed large above the door, as if announcing the predator who lurked within. The outdoor seating was empty, the chairs upside down on the tables and locked into place by a long, green cord. I hopped out of the truck and crossed the almost deserted street, noticing a Mercedes sedan parked on the side with the restaurant's name on its license plate.

I ignored the 'Closed' sign, pushed at the glass

door, and with a slight shove, it popped open. The restaurant was vacant, save for a man standing behind the bar cleaning glasses.

"Not open tonight," he called over to me. "Come back tomorrow."

"Here to see Sergio."

"For what?" a second voice called from somewhere beyond the door to the kitchen. It sounded gruff, laced with the kind of authority I had heard from the younger Costa.

"Just a few questions," I called back, hoping he wouldn't need any more convincing. Back in his past life, Sergio Costa would've sent his heavy hitters out ahead of him to work me over first to see whether I was worthy of his time, but those days appeared long gone.

Sergio Costa stepped out into the main eatery, wiping his hands on a cloth as if he'd been washing the dishes himself. Maybe he had, but the dominant man I remembered from our previous meeting appeared to be gone. The man standing before me was a far cry from that long-ago version.

He'd aged considerably, his previous dark hair replaced with the familiar grey that seemed to wait for the best of us. His face had also lost its previous confidence, now mostly hidden beneath a thinning white beard. This Sergio Costa was but a shadow of his former self. He had been a large man, an intimidating figure for anyone who crossed him, but now he was hunched over and walking slower, although his broad shoulders still looked strong enough to throw a heavy left hook.

"Jack Valentine," I offered, walking towards him with my hand outstretched.

Sergio attempted a friendly expression, shaking hands with me and leading me towards a nearby table. That was another surprise. Before, he would've asked me a bunch of questions to satisfy his conscience. Guilty men always did. But there were no questions, no interrogation, and no threats. He was as accepting as any normal man would be.

"Is this about the article in 'Delish'?"

The name of the magazine brought back an instant torrent of dread for me, remembering Claire had read it religiously for the entirety of our relationship. Sergio thought I was a reporter. The idea briefly humored me, and I didn't answer until we were both seated, just in case he changed his mind.

"Not quite." His demeanor until that point had been accommodating, almost welcoming, but something told me things were about to head south. "I need to ask you a few questions about your son, Mark Costa."

The wall instantly went up. Whatever welcome Sergio Costa had offered me had been taken back and thrown out.

"Did Marco send you?" His voice had turned dry, almost harsh, but he kept his tone low, a growl worthy of a wolf. "What does he want?"

"It's for a case I'm working on." I realized that he might have thought I was a cop, perhaps karma from a long-ago incident finally catching up. His face grew pale for just an instant, but it wasn't long before the Sergio of old showed up.

"You with the PD?"

"Private investigator."

"You working for Marco? Is that it?"

"I am."

"I've told the cops all I know about that robbery. They called me, and I told them it wasn't me." He leaned back in his chair. "I didn't break into my son's apartment, I didn't target him, and it wasn't me that made off with whatever filth he held there. I didn't take the fifty thousand dollars from him. It insulted me that he thought I would stoop that low for that small amount of cash."

If Sergio knew about the stolen laptop, he didn't show it. "But you know about the robbery."

"Of course I know about it. The cops called here last week, asking me offensive questions." He paused to catch his breath, leaned in a little closer, and whispered, "Do you know what that scumbag did to me?"

"Convinced you to give up your company?"

That seemed to shock him back down to earth, and he sat back in his seat.

"He told you that, huh?" His eyes squinted a little, as if to see a little deeper inside me. "Did he tell you everything?"

"Everything? Probably not. He told me as much as I needed to know."

Five years ago, Sergio Costa would've been the kind of man to have me dragged out back and beaten to a pulp just for having the audacity to walk into his place of business without prior arrangement and fire off questions. Sitting down at a table with him would've been out of the question.

"Just how much do you know? I'm curious as to why he'd hire someone like you for a cash robbery. I think he must've lost more than cash, something pretty valuable." He rolled his tongue around his mouth as he thought about his next words. "Perhaps something he didn't tell the cops about?"

"I'm just here about the theft of the money," I said, hoping to get things back on track. "I wanted to chat about whether you know anyone that works in his building."

"It wasn't me. How clear do I have to be?" He hesitated, squinting at me again with those piercing black eyes of his. "You really think that I would break into Marco's apartment to steal 50K?"

"Mark—"

"His name is Marco." He interrupted me. "I hate this Western name, Mark. He was born Marco, he was raised Marco, and his name is Marco. I expect you to call him Marco when you talk about him."

"Your son," I nodded. "Marco was robbed, and he's hired me to find out what the police couldn't. So, can anyone vouch for your personal whereabouts on the night of the 5th of May?"

"I was at home watching the Cubs game."

"Can anyone verify that?"

"I used to watch the games with Marco, but I haven't done that for a very long time." He groaned and then looked away. "I used to pitch for a Triple-A minor league team. I taught that idiot son of mine everything there was to know about baseball, but his arm was too soft. He didn't make it to the big leagues because he's weak, in his body and in his mind. He couldn't even hold down a spot in his minor league team. He said he quit, but I know he was dropped. The coach chose someone else over him. He was useless as a baseball player, and he's an even worse businessman."

My years in this profession taught me that lying comes naturally to some people, but yet, there was one thing a person could never fully control—their eyes. Peering into someone's eyes at the moment they're lying is a key to knowing the truth. Both Sergio and I knew he wasn't telling me the truth about his whereabouts on the night in question, and yet he unashamedly continued with the lie. My stare told him everything I was thinking.

"You didn't answer my question," I stated. "Can anyone verify where you were on the 5th of May?"

"If I wanted fifty thousand dollars, I could get it by other means, and nobody would ever know." He leaned forward again. "Do I need to remind you about what I can do? Do you even know who I am?"

Whatever questions I still had wouldn't be asked that day. Sergio Costa stood as the other man stepped out from behind the bar.

"We're done here." Sergio's tone conveyed the finality of the conversation. "I had nothing to do with the break-in at that scum's apartment."

He turned and walked away, not bothering to wait for a reply. The other man waited, eyeballing me until I rose from my chair and headed back out into the cold.

While I didn't get the answers I came looking for, I did get enough for me to know that Sergio Costa wasn't in the clear. He remained at the very top of my list of suspects.

CHAPTER 7

CASEY WAS waiting out in front of Mark Costa's apartment building, and I'd pulled alongside the parked cars, temporarily halting traffic behind me.

"How'd you do last night with Sergio Costa?" Casey asked as she climbed into my truck. There was a brief gush of cold as the door opened, but thankfully the heater made short work of it once she was inside. Once she'd buckled her seatbelt, I kept driving, allowing the traffic to flow again.

"Our meeting couldn't have gone any smoother," I exaggerated. "It was a laugh a minute. Sergio should've been a comedian."

She recognized the sarcasm in my tone and smiled. "That good, huh?"

"That good. It's always a joy to see a father's expression turn icy at the mention of his son's name."

"I'm guessing he didn't come out and confess then? Did he tell you he had the laptop?"

"Not quite. He didn't mention the laptop, and he didn't seem to know about it. And, of course, Sergio Costa had a rock-solid alibi for that night, the sort that could only be verified by himself."

"What a surprise."

"He claimed he was at home alone watching a ball game. Then he told me how good he used to be as a pitcher and how he was disappointed that his son had such a weak arm," I said, maneuvering the truck through the traffic. "How about you? Get the USB drive from our man who's 'Russian' to help out?"

"Enough Dad jokes." She smiled and held up the USB. "Ivan was happy to help without Costa around. I wouldn't call him relaxed, but he was a lot more talkative."

"And last night? Were your friends able to tell you much about Costa?"

"Blunt is one word for it. I spoke to five people, and not a single positive thing was said about Mark Costa." Her tone matched my mood. "They told me there were rumors that he used to run a dog-fighting ring, rumors that he bribed city officials, and rumors that he hired heavies to beat down on any rival that challenged him. But, of course, all these things have remained rumors, and no charges have ever been filed against him."

"How about the murdered man?"

"Not a lot of information about him yet, but I'm still building the file. Name was Michael Hoffman, hard worker in the construction industry. Never married, but had a long-term partner and has adult children. No social media presence and not much information available on the internet. Police report was brief, and his funeral had about fifty in attendance."

"Let's keep working that angle and see if we can find a connection between Hoffman and any of our suspects."

"Right," Casey made a note on her phone. "Where to next, boss?"

"We're going to chat with the cleaner," I said. "She may be able to tell us a thing or two about the security guard at the building."

Casey pulled out her laptop from her bag and uploaded the video footage from the USB as I continued heading towards the Walmart where Lauren Taylor worked her second job. Just the prospect of working two jobs had me wondering about cleaning a wealthy person's apartment and being surrounded by temptation, but I quickly flushed the idea. If a person was struggling that much and giving in to that temptation, they wouldn't bother with a second job.

After twenty-five minutes of early morning traffic, I pulled into the outdoor lot and parked, and Casey and I made our way inside. It was early, but some of Walmart's best customers were already there—people in pajamas, drunk people on their way home after a big night out, and workers stopping in before another day in office-life.

"My friend's cat lost its tail last week, so we took him to Walmart," Casey said as we walked in the front doors and nodded to the greeter. "They were the biggest re-tailer we could think of."

I chuckled as we searched the aisles. After walking through half the store, we eventually found our intended target stacking shelves in the canned soup section. Her perfectly lined up stack of canned tomato soup almost looked like an Andy Warhol painting.

"Lauren Taylor?" Casey asked.

The woman turned in surprise. She looked different from when we saw her the day before— here, the mid-thirties woman looked tired and rushed with her brunette hair up in a messy ponytail.

"Yes?" A faint blush rose in her cheeks. She

looked up at me. "Oh, you're the investigators from Mark Costa's place yesterday. How did you know I worked here?"

"We investigate. That's what we're good at," Casey smiled. "Do you mind if we ask you a few quick questions about Mark Costa? It won't take long."

The woman looked from Casey to me and back again, concern in her eyes. A shopper passed between us, paused to grab a can of pumpkin soup, gave the three of us a quick eyeball, then continued on.

"Is there a problem?" Lauren asked with a distinct hesitation in her tone once we were alone in the aisle again. "The police have already questioned me. I didn't really have anything that could help them. I told them what I knew about the place, but I was nowhere near it that night. I told the police everything I know. I only clean the place a few times a week, and there's really nothing more to tell. I wasn't there that day, but I came in the next morning to clean the apartment. When I arrived, the police were already there, and instead of getting to work, I found myself being questioned for more than fifty minutes. And Mark didn't pay me for a second of it."

"Police can certainly be thorough," Casey added in a nurturing tone. "We were wondering how long you've been cleaning Mark Costa's apartment?"

"I've cleaned his apartment for around five months, but I've worked for the cleaning company for about a year."

"Have you ever found anything out of the ordinary in his apartment?"

She tilted her head a little. "Out of the ordinary?"

"You know, something that seemed out of place." Casey knew that it was a long shot, since some people's apartments were virtually filled with things out of the ordinary. "Anything that seemed a little 'off.' Anything you can tell us is going to help."

"It's a pretty standard apartment. I clean three others in the same building, and they all look fairly similar. All of the men are cold, lifeless, money-hungry professionals, and they all live the same way. They're all single men, all professionals, and all have the standard messes." She shifted her stance a little. "Actually, Mark's is probably one of the cleaner ones compared to the others."

"Do you ever find lots of empty alcohol bottles, drugs, that sort of thing?" I asked.

She looked a little shocked at that, but I couldn't detect any deception from her or any nerves that indicated she was trying to hide something. She was either very controlled or purely innocent.

"I found a small bag of white powder in one of the other apartments, but never in Mark's. Just the standard dishes, dust, and laundry for him." She looked over her shoulder. "I don't have a lot to do with Mark. The few times I see him there, he's shouting at me, telling me what a bad job I'm doing. He says things about my age, and how being a cleaner is such a bad job for a woman in their thirties. He treats me like a loser, but I'm not a loser. I work two jobs and go to night school. He's just a nasty piece of work."

"Is there anything you can think of that might help us find the person responsible?" Casey pressed. "Anything at all? Perhaps you could tell us about the security team in the building?"

She thought long and hard about the question. "The big Russian always seemed nice to me. Ivan

Pushkin. He has no social skills, but it seems like his heart is in the right place."

Casey and I exchanged a look before Casey continued. "Have you ever seen evidence of anyone else visiting the apartment? Perhaps two wine glasses left on the table, or two sets of take-out containers?"

She again shook her head. "As far as I know, he spends his time alone. And when he has 'company,' it's paid for."

I figured we were done and went to thank her for talking with us, when she suddenly had a light bulb moment. Her face almost lit up as something came to mind.

"You know something else?" Casey asked, beating me to the punch.

"I don't know if I should say anything. It's his private life." She crossed her arms across her chest but then continued. "There's this girl who I saw once. She was coming out just as I arrived, and I thought she might have been a girlfriend of his."

"Do you have a name?"

"Millie? Mandy?" She looked up towards the ceiling, trying to recall the evasive memory. "It was a few months ago. I only saw her the one time, but something told me she'd been back several more times."

"How can you tell?" I asked.

"I could smell her perfume in the air. It was fairly distinctive."

"Nothing else?"

"Not evidence of her presence, no." And then, as if discovering the secrets to the universe, Lauren snapped her fingers, remembering something relevant to our cause. "Mindy, that's it. Her name was Mindy."

"Everything ok, Lauren?" a voice called from behind us. I turned to see a man wearing the same Walmart uniform but with a name badge that announced his managerial position. Lauren looked over Casey's shoulder and gave a thumbs up.

"All good," she called back. "Just helping these customers."

The man offered a fake smile and disappeared back behind the shelves, but I could still see his shoulder at the edge of the shelf. He was watching us, or more specifically, he was watching Lauren.

"That's my manager," Lauren whispered. "Sorry, but I have to get back to work. He doesn't like us wasting time."

"Under a bit of pressure?" Casey said.

"Yeah, they work us to the bone in this store."

"You don't have to put up with poor treatment," Casey said. "You could stand up to him."

"I wish." She looked pensive. "My father was a Union Manager for the Building and Trade Union. He unionized a lot of workers, and he'd do anything for the rights of the workers. And I'll tell you now, he never would've stood for the way we're treated here. He would've had this whole store striking within a day."

"Unions aren't always the best thing for workers," Casey said. "But we always need good leaders to stand up for the little guy. You could do that without a union."

"I'd lose my job," she said. "The people that own Walmart are all billionaires, and here we are, worried whether we've taken twenty-five minutes for a lunch break instead of twenty."

The man appeared around the end of the aisle

again.

"You've been a great help," I said, facing Lauren but loud enough for the man to hear. "Best service I've ever received in a Walmart. If all Walmart staff were like you, this would be the best place in the world."

"Thank you, Lauren," Casey said quieter. "You've been very helpful."

We both waved another thank you. Having people like that to interview made things so much easier in my line of work. They were forthcoming with information and freely offered up things I could spend weeks trying to find. Casey followed me back out into the parking lot, and we didn't speak again until we were both in the truck.

"Mindy?" Casey asked, and I wondered the same. "That could be our mystery person known as 'M' on the bracelet. Costa's ex-wife's name is Sandra, and although he said it was a misprint on the bracelet, I think it's pretty clear that he's lying now."

"Just another thing Mark Costa failed to tell us. I wonder how much more he's really hiding." I fired up the truck, then simply sat and stared out through the windshield. Doubts about the case set in again. There was something off about the man paying us and his repeated attempts to pull the wool over our eyes. If anything, it was frustration that clouded my thoughts.

"I'm sorry for this," Casey said, effectively shocking me back into the cabin of the pick-up.

"Sorry?" I asked. "Sorry for what?"

"For bringing Mark Costa to you."

"You didn't bring him to me. And I sure as hell didn't have to take him on. That decision is on me." I didn't like this part of her, but some people have that quality in their nature, and Casey was one of those people who always saw the well-being of others as her own duty.

"Yes, but he was my brother's friend, and you attended the memorial. If I didn't ask you to come for support—"

I held up a hand and stopped her mid-sentence. "One has nothing to do with the other, and it's not like we're suffering here. He's frustrating, but we've experienced a lot worse than Mark Costa in our time." I could see her defenses drop a little. "This is just another case, and in a day or two, we'll get to the bottom of things and move on to the next one."

"Thank you, Jack," she said, and without another hesitation, I pushed my truck into gear and pulled out of the parking lot.

"Where to now?" Casey asked.

"Back to ask our old pal some more questions."

CHAPTER 8

I FOUGHT through traffic towards where I knew Mark Costa would be basking in his favorite environment—surrounded by those who would bend to his every beck and call. The main office of his property development firm was located almost twenty-five miles south, and the drive gave Casey and I time to continue discussing the case in more detail.

"You think she's his girlfriend?" Casey asked as we drove. "Maybe a side piece?"

"Girlfriend, no." I could tell from Mark Costa's demeanor that he liked the ladies. He had an ex-wife and children he didn't appear to care for, and when adding up all that information, it led to a simple answer for me. "A guy like Mark Costa won't want to be tied down by another relationship when he's so detached from his previous one. He's a player."

"A player and narcissist," Casey agreed. "I'll be interested to hear what he has to say on the subject."

I didn't answer right away, my mind traveling back to the memorial for Casey's foster-brother. There was something that had been bothering me, but up until that moment, I couldn't quite put my finger on what it was. Sitting in traffic, it hit me.

"Has Mark Costa attended any memorials before?" Casey took a moment to think back.

"Never, but this was a big one. Ten years. I've

invited him every year, but this was the first time he's attended one."

"Why this year?" I asked, the thought building into something more significant in my mind.

Casey again took her time, staring blankly through the windshield. It took her a long time to answer, perhaps caught up in another memory of Rhys. "You think he came for us? You think he knew I'd be there, and when he saw you, he took advantage of that?"

"It makes sense," I began. "He didn't exactly have a lot to contribute. He sat silently for the majority and passed up the opportunity to speak when it was presented to him, and he doesn't seem like the sentimental type. Also, he'd just been robbed a few days before and was in the middle of searching for the stolen laptop. I doubt he would've found the time, if he was there for any other reason."

From what I recalled, out of all the people that had attended the memorial, there were only three people Mark had actually interacted with—Casey upon his arrival, a girl who'd offered him his beverage, and me. And he'd only spoken to me once we were both outside in the front yard.

The rest of the time, Mark kept to himself, appearing caught up in his own distractions, whether it was staring at his cell or watching as others interacted. He didn't go out of his way to offer support, and the others didn't appear too interested in speaking with him.

We drove in silence for the remainder of the trip, Casey watching the passing traffic through her side window. I could only imagine the emotions that had been ignited by taking on this job from a man linked to Rhys. It made me question taking on the case yet again. I hated how personal this was becoming, more for her sake than mine.

The parking lot next to Mark Costa's current construction site was almost completely full of work vehicles. I parked down the street, and when I climbed out of the truck, I felt the cold of the day immediately. Several power tools were running somewhere beyond the fence, and a couple of male voices were shouting above the noise. I immediately recognized one of the voices as our current employer.

The fences around the construction site were high and covered in mesh-wrapping, and a number of signs were posted along the exterior. We followed the fence around the exterior until we came to the main gates. We stepped through the front entrance and saw there was a standard portable building in one corner, a small sign in the window marking it as the 'Site Office.'

As we walked towards the site office, we found Mark walking towards the front door. He looked surprised to see us, but save for a tiny sliver of shock, he quickly returned to his usual arrogant self.

"All solved, I hope," he said. "I don't want to see you here otherwise."

It was the smugness that irritated me more than anything, and I felt like slamming the job down his throat. But professionalism was a word I respected and thus held my own emotions back. For the time being, anyway. "Not quite. We need to ask you a few more questions."

He hesitated as he considered the request, giving Casey a quick up-and-down as he held the moment. "Ok," he finally said. "Follow me."

Mark Costa turned and led us inside. The site office had a small reception area, with two offices sitting side-by-side at the other end. One of these doors was closed, with a nameplate announcing its occupant.

Mark Costa
CEO and Executive Director

The titles irritated me again, the guy needing every possible opportunity to remind people who he was, as if anyone had any time to forget. He led the way through the door, and then sat behind his large desk and waved at the two chairs facing him. "Sit down."

"Who's Mindy?" I asked without bothering to wait. He paused as if I'd caught him off guard, then looked out past me towards the pretty blonde receptionist before I could say anything else.

"Cleo, would you hold my calls for five minutes?"

As the receptionist nodded back to him, she stood and closed the door, separating herself from a man who loved the attention.

He only spoke again once the door was closed, as if needing to ensure any revealed secrets remained locked in the room.

"How did you find out about Mindy?" He was caught off guard, and his entire demeanor became defensive. "Who told you about her?"

"We found her by following our leads," I said. "I'll ask again—who's Mindy?"

He started at me while considering my question, his index fingers pressed together as he sat back in his seat. "Those leads won't help you." He was almost whispering, as if speaking to himself, before adding,

"She's nobody."

"If she has access to your apartment, then she's somebody, and if she's somebody, then we need to question her," Casey said. "If we're going to find out what the cops didn't, then we need to look at everything. That means we need to look into everyone who has access to your apartment."

"Have you spoken to that stupid Russian security guard?" He questioned.

"Yes."

"And the cleaner—what's her name?"

"Lauren Taylor," I replied. "Yes, we've spoken to her. And our investigations have confirmed that someone else has access to your apartment. So I'll ask a third time, who is Mindy?"

"Mindy is not part of this case." He was deflecting, refusing to answer the simple question. "She's got nothing to do with this."

"I beg to differ." I stood, walked to the window, and looked out across the work-site. He didn't appear to think I would walk out, but I could feel his eyes burning into the back of my head. I continued without turning back. "You came to us with this problem of yours, and yet every time we ask you a question, you do your best to try and lead us away from the truth. Now, why would that be?"

The room was silent behind me, Casey sitting patiently before Mark, the two of them staring at each other. When I eventually turned back to him, Mark finally spoke.

"Mindy Fox is what you might call 'hired help.'"

"A hooker?" I asked, casting any niceties aside. I'd had enough of his deflection and wanted straight answers.

"Not quite." He shuffled in his seat uncomfortably, doing his best to try and find the right words that would somehow save face for him. He could see my expression and knew my patience had almost run out entirely. "We met on a website called 'MissMatch'. They connect young ladies looking for rich men, regardless of age. We were a good match."

The silence descended again as Mark fell quiet, perhaps wondering whether he'd made the right decision to share his secret.

It was Casey who broke the silence. "A sugar-daddy website?"

"It was the right fit for me." He held his hands up in surrender as if to confirm his true intentions. "She had what I wanted, and I had what she wanted. She's twenty-one, and she can do what she likes. I'm rich and I can do what I like. It was a perfect match."

"How long has this girl been around?"

"About five months now." He sat forward in his chair and dropped his hands on the desk. "Mindy is what I consider my private business. I've never told her about the laptop, nor anything else about what happened between my father and me. She comes around to keep me company, and I give her expensive gifts in return. It's an amicable relationship. We both get what we want out of our time together."

"Do you two ever go out and public?" I asked. Costa looked surprised at that.

"A few times. Why should that matter?"

Casey chimed in to prove the point I hadn't made yet. "If you two were seen together, then whoever decided to rob you may have contacted Mindy and hired her to help. You did say she was hired help after all. She could've sold you out for money."

"She's not part of this case," Costa snapped back. "She wouldn't cross me like that." And then, as if to convince himself, he added, "No way, not to me. She's—"

"On a website to offer her kindness for financial gain," I interrupted. "A gold digger, so to speak. That means she has a price for just about anything, including sleeping with you."

That final part felt good to throw at him, and I could see the sting in his eyes.

"You've got her wrong," Mark tried. "She lives with her sick Mom. Takes care of her. She's a good girl who just wants to earn money to look after her family."

"And you've met her sick mother?" I asked. "Perhaps you've seen photos of the mother?"

"Well, no, but why would I? That's not what we do." A look of realization washed over his face. "You think she's lying to me to get sympathy. Look, I don't care about her personal life. I don't care if she's dating anyone else. When we're together, we're focused on each other. That's what matters."

I didn't need to hear any more, especially him justifying why he went to that type of website in search of company. All I needed was the girl's contact details.

"How can we get in touch with this girl?" I asked.

"For what? There's no need to speak with her. I told you she wasn't part of this case."

I wasn't going to give him a chance to try and deflect this time. "Her phone number and address," I repeated.

"I don't have her address," he conceded. "But I know she works a few shifts at a Starbucks. She's mentioned her work a few times. She's trying to become an actress and just trying to get ahead."

I leaned forward and pushed a notepad towards him. Mark looked down at it before finally giving in.

"Fine." He wrote for a few seconds, then dropped the pen down with a clunk before tearing the top sheet off. Mark held it out to me, and I could see he wasn't happy about it.

I unfolded the sheet and looked down at his writing, making sure that he'd delivered what we'd come for. Her cell number was written beneath the words, Starbucks. South Longwood and W103rd.

"Wasn't so hard now, was it?" I said. And then, as a gentle reminder, I added, "Just remember we're on your team. We don't need any more of these constant hindrances that keep popping up, so if you want this case solved, help us."

I turned to leave, and Casey followed close behind. We left Mark sitting in his office and headed back out into the cold of the day. Casey and I climbed back into the truck. With the note stuffed into my shirt pocket, I didn't hesitate to get out of there. Getting some distance between Mark Costa and us was the only way to calm the anger that had been steadily building up over the previous two days.

"Why's everything so difficult with that guy?" I snapped. I'd begun to think that it was just in his character. Some people were built to create waves, and Mark Costa happened to be a master at it.

"I don't think he does it intentionally to deceive you," Casey offered as I rejoined the traffic. "A man like that just has too many skeletons in his closet, and he's got to be concerned about which skeleton will fall out if he opens the door a little too far."

My mind felt exhausted, and a good cup of coffee would be just the thing to help. Starbucks seemed like the perfect answer, and I turned the pick-up towards our next target, ready to move towards completing this case.

We were getting closer to the truth, but I wondered how many more obstacles lay before us.

CHAPTER 9

THE STARBUCKS heater must've been working overtime because the hot air that punched me in the face as I walked through the front door was overpowering and unwelcome. But despite the attack of hot air at the entrance, the rest of the store was pleasant, and there was no denying the sweet smell hanging in the air. There was a comfort to the smell of coffee, a reassurance that another hit of caffeine wasn't far away.

There were five people lined up. One woman was taking orders behind the counter, while two others were busy making ridiculous variations of a simple caffeine hit. They looked overworked and tired, with strained expressions from repeating the same words all day. Thankfully, they wore name tags, and I saw Mindy was one of the girls handling the serving duties.

She looked a lot younger than I'd envisioned and wondered about the man paying for this girl's after-hours services. Despite her age, she looked almost exactly how I assumed she would, right down to her blonde hair which was secured by an oversized comb clasp, holding it up in a large clump on the back of her head.

It wasn't Mindy who served me, but she did take a sideways glance at me, perhaps feeling my eyes on her. I didn't want us getting off on the wrong foot and so leaned a little over the counter.

"Mindy, my name is Jack Valentine. My partner and I," I began and turned a little to point at Casey, who waved with a friendly smile, then continued with, "were wondering if we could have a quick chat?"

She looked a little startled when I began the conversation with her name but must've realized she had it displayed for all to see before answering me.

"You a cop?" It was a standard response in my line of work, especially amongst younger people who watched a lot of movies.

"No," I shook my head. "It's regarding Mark Costa."

This time panic did flash across her face, and for a moment, I wondered whether I had in fact stumbled on the guilty party after all. Perhaps she did steal the money and the laptop, and she wasn't expecting a random stranger to come seeking her out. But despite my concerns, she surprised me with her sudden change in mood.

"I'm due for a break in like five minutes. Can you wait?"

I nodded and stood aside to wait for my order. Once the other girl called my name out, I grabbed the two cups of joe along with a blueberry muffin and joined Casey at one of the tables near the darkest corner of the establishment. Just as she always did, Casey reserved my seat near the wall, knowing full well that I preferred to have my back to the wall and a complete view of a room whenever out in public.

We sat and made small talk, each of us stealing the occasional glance over to the counter as the girls continued to serve the never-ending stream of customers that seemed to arrive out of nowhere. I enjoyed the strong smell of coffee, but the constant chatter was too loud for me to relax.

"Do you think she'll do a runner?" Casey asked.

"No. We've got her where she works. She's cornered," I looked at Mindy. "She knows if we can find out where she works, we can find out where she lives."

Ten minutes later, Mindy walked over to us and sat down, sucking an iced coffee through a straw.

"This must be important if Mark sent you to my workplace."

"He didn't send us," I began. "He hired us to find the person who robbed his apartment a few nights ago. We're private investigators, and we're following all the leads we have regarding this crime. Those leads have led us here."

The same look of apprehension drifted across her face, and this time, she must've noticed I saw it because she immediately sipped her drink again. I wondered whether it was her subconsciously shielding herself from us.

"You're not under suspicion," Casey offered. "Jack just has a few questions, that's all."

"Makes me nervous talking about him," she whispered, setting her cup down. "What we do isn't common knowledge."

"Nervous talking about Mark?" Casey continued. "Why?"

"He's not the nicest guy I know. Tends to treat me like one of his cars—just there to be used when he needs it. I'm worried that if I do something to offend him, he'll cut me off and never contact me again."

"Then why continue seeing him?"

Mindy looked up at that, as if expecting us to know the answer. "Because growing up in my neighborhood didn't exactly bring many worthwhile opportunities, if you know what I mean."

"He pays you?" I asked.

"Not exactly." She looked over her shoulder and lowered her voice. "It began with earrings, you know, nothing too over the top. The next time, it was a ring. Then a handbag."

"I'm guessing we're talking brand names here?"

"The best, yeah. Thousands of dollars' worth." She kept her voice low. "But he never followed up on the gifts."

"Followed up?"

"The moment he handed them to me was the moment he forgot about them. So, I began to sell them and used the money for more worthwhile things."

"Such as your sick mother?"

"He told you about that, huh?" She looked sheepish. "Listen, don't tell Mark, but my mother's alive and well, living in Florida. That was something that a friend suggested I say, to try and get sympathy from him. It's not like he actually cares about me or my life."

"So what do you really need the money for then?"

"Well, right now, I'm saving up to move to Hollywood. I want to be an actress." Her eyes grew distant as the words left her lips. She sucked down her drink again. "And I enjoy partying. You've got to do it when you're young. My mother always told me to get out there and live hard while I'm young, because when you're old, life becomes really monotonous. You've got to create memories."

"What sort of partying?" I questioned. "Hard drugs?"

"Some pills." She shrugged as if it was nothing. "I like to hit the underground raves."

I nodded. She had the motive to steal the fifty-thousand in cash from the safe, but it didn't explain why the laptop was also missing.

"Are you a supplier?" I probed.

"What? No. No way." She tensed up. "I just get enough for me. I have a friend who deals, and they give me some. Is that what you're here for? To find my dealer? Am I in trouble?"

"Nothing like that." Casey reached her hand out and calmed Mindy down. Casey's calming influence was invaluable in these situations. "We have no interest in your weekend activities. We're only interested in finding what was stolen."

"Does Mark have a temper?" I questioned. It drew our suspect back to the conversation.

"A temper?"

"Has he ever hit you? Or been violent towards you?"

She looked shocked at that. "Uh-uh, no way. He knows I wouldn't stand for that. Perhaps with others from his past he has, but not with me." I believed her and could see from the look on her face that she was telling the truth. "He's rude and arrogant, but I put up with it."

"Mindy, forgive me for saying this, but he doesn't sound like the sort of guy who you'd go out of your way to be with," Casey said. "Not when there must've been a whole host of other more suitable choices on that website."

Casey didn't mean to embarrass her, but the blush

that bloomed low in her cheeks and continued to brighten as it made its way across her face was undeniable. It wasn't something she was overly proud of.

"He wasn't supposed to tell anyone about the website."

"We forced it out of him," I said. "I like to know everything about a person before I climb into bed with them." The blush grew more fiercely. "Proverbially speaking," I added.

"Not my finest hour," she whispered. "I only did it because my friend Becky told me about the site and how she made a lot of money from dating this old guy she met on there. She only talked to him, and she didn't have to do anything physical."

"We're not here to judge," I said. She sounded defensive, and I wanted to calm her down a little.

"Does he ever speak about anyone else?" Casey steered the conversation back on track. "Any enemies or people that are getting under his skin?"

"He's more private about his past than you might imagine. He's only mentioned his kids once, and I don't even know their names. And he's never mentioned his ex-wife. Sometimes we do… physical things…" she drew a breath and sighed. "But other times, he just talks. He talks to me like a therapist sometimes, and he tells me things. Personal things." I couldn't imagine Mark getting personal with anybody. "Like how this one person gives him a hard time, constantly trying to undercut him and steal business away from his company."

My ears pricked up at that. It sounded like another person who might have a reason to rob him. I waited for a more opportune time to cut in, but Casey knew what she was doing.

"He must have a few people like that in his life."

"From what I've heard, there's one guy that's really bad."

"Do you have a name?"

She looked over her shoulder again and then leaned forward. "As far as I know, it's just Julian Wright."

The name rang a bell. He was on Costa's list of conflicts over the past year, but it was more than that. I couldn't quite place the exact circumstances when I'd heard his name. I was going to be searching my memory banks on that one, although I knew Casey would be doing the same.

Before I could ask anything else, Mindy looked at her phone, saw the time, and grabbed her beverage. "I have to get back to it."

She rose to leave, but before she could, Casey asked, "Do you have a number we can reach you on, in case we have any more questions?"

We already had her cell number from Mark, but it was worth confirming it with her.

"Ok," she answered, and when Casey slid a pen and business card over to her, Mindy leaned down and began to write. A moment later, she was back behind the counter taking orders.

We both finished our drinks and made our way out, flashing Mindy a quick smile as we passed the counter. Once we were back in the truck, I fired up the engine but remained idling in the spot, running the past couple of days through my head again.

The list of suspects only seemed to be growing larger.

CHAPTER 10

"LACK OF motive is the only reason we're not searching Mindy's apartment right now," I said as we drove back to the office. "I can understand why she would've taken the cash, but the laptop? Sergio didn't appear to know the laptop was missing, so he didn't set this up. So the question remains, who asked her to take it?"

"If she took it," Casey added. "We know she wasn't mentioned in the police report, they didn't even know she existed, but I'm not convinced. If she took the fifty thousand, we would've seen some evidence of it. A new car, a new piece of jewelry, or—"

"More drugs," I added. "She said she was a raver. Maybe that's where she'll spend the money."

"Hang on." Casey scanned her phone, flicking through various websites. "There's an underground rave happening this weekend. We could follow her there?"

"And listen to that music?" I laughed. "No thanks. I like having my eardrums intact. Let's scope out her apartment tomorrow, see who comes and goes. If we can see someone who looks like they're buying drugs, then maybe we have our girl."

"Ok. That's tomorrow. What about the rest of today?"

"I haven't followed up the other leads yet, and Mindy mentioned Julian Wright, who was already on the list. I'm going to have a chat with him and see where that leads us. Could be the motive we're after."

A quick search on Casey's phone found everything we needed to know about Julian Wright. That's where investigations had changed so much over the past decade—what used to take call after call after call, pressing contacts and probing for information, could now be done from the passenger seat of a car, typing away on the tiny super-computer that also doubled as a cell phone. It was easier, but that didn't mean I liked it. I liked having contacts, talking to people, exchanging information, wheeling and dealing for insider knowledge. But the world had changed, and if I didn't change with it, I would just end up a grumpy old man on the front porch, whittling wood and screaming about the ideals of yesteryear. As much as I didn't like it, times had changed and I had to accept it.

We discussed searching Mindy's apartment again but agreed that it wasn't worth the risk of getting caught for breaking and entering until we were more certain.

I dropped Casey at the office to search for anything on Mindy Fox that could establish a motive, and I continued on towards a construction site in Arlington Heights.

Julian Wright's company had won a substantial building contract with a supermarket giant, and from what Casey had found online, that deal had led to an additional five development sites. They were big contracts and it was big money, in the hundreds of millions. Notably, amongst the defeated bids for the contracts was the Costa organization. I could only imagine how Mark Costa must have taken the loss at the time.

It was almost midday by the time I reached the construction site's outer perimeter fence and I parked in amongst other vehicles, each just as banged up as my own. My old girl looked like it belonged, and it reminded me of a moment almost fifteen years ago when I had joined a construction crew. There's a certain appeal about donning some coveralls and getting your hands dirty while building something substantial, leaving behind a legacy of your work, something to live on after you're gone. The camaraderie on the site was unmatched, and despite the long hours, I had looked forward to hitting the tools each day.

The building site didn't appear to be any supermarket I'd ever seen, and a quick scan of one of the nearby billboards identified this site as the new corporate headquarters for the group. No wonder it looked like a multi-story office block.

As I jumped out of the truck, the cold once again hit me. There were men with tools walking every which way, all of them wearing hardhats and yelling various obscenities at each other in jovial voices.

"Hey," a voice called from somewhere over near one of the gates leading inside. I looked around and found the voice's owner, a middle-aged man that would struggle not to break a sweat going up a small flight of stairs. His face was the color of tomatoes, and I recalled hearing that a person with a red-face could signify heart problems. "Can't be onsite without safety gear."

I groaned, reminding myself that the world we once knew was long gone. "I'm here to see Mr.

Wright," I called back, taking a step or two in his direction.

"Julian? He's over in the cafe," the man said, pointing to somewhere behind me. I turned and saw a little Mom and Pop corner diner across the street.

"Thanks," I called back, but the man had already disappeared again, no doubt to somewhere where he could spot the next unfortunate soul who mistakenly entered his lot without the correct safety gear.

The street was lined with work vehicles on both sides, and yet there was virtually no traffic. Once inside the cafe, there were half a dozen workmen standing by the counter, with several tables scattered around the open area of the small business. Four of the tables were occupied by two or more people, but seated right at the back, in a position I had always favored, was a bulky man, a laptop opened before him, a white mug next to it.

Despite having the same job title, Julian Wright appeared a lot different than my current employer.

From what I'd seen, Mark Costa lacked the natural ability to demand respect from his peers. He was like a rich kid with a limitless credit card, flashing it around to as many people as possible. He ordered respect from his employees because he could never earn it any other way.

Sitting at the table in the shop was a man who appeared to be the opposite—he earned the respect of his team, his own confidence held in check through years of experience. I could tell he was a hard-head, but there wasn't a doubt in my mind that the man could also sit down for a drink with the boys and share war stories over a cold one.

He was sitting alone, reading something on the

laptop, occasionally looking out into the cafe. I didn't bother trying to dress the situation up and walked up to his table.

"Mr. Wright, Jack Valentine. I was wondering if we could talk." He looked up, and I could immediately see he had the hunger for success lurking in his eyes, the way most successful businessmen did. I wasn't sure how things would go, so I added a little something I hoped would turn the tables in my favor. "It's about Mark Costa."

Just as I had hoped, the final addition worked its magic almost instantly. His half-grin completely disappeared as he heard the name, his face contorting with dread. His reaction reminded me of Sergio's, and I was becoming used to people's reaction at the mention of Mark Costa's name.

"Don't tell me you chose to work for that prick," he said. "He sent you over here about the Morrison St. development? You tell that sack of—"

"I'm not here to harass you." That brought him back to earth a little. "I'm trying to follow some leads for a burglary."

"A burglary? You a cop?"

"I'm not a cop. I'm a private investigator."

I pointed at the chair opposite him. He nodded in response and then leaned forward as I sat. His eyes locked onto mine, judging my reaction to his next question.

"Must've been something valuable that was stolen." He took a sip from his mug and sat back; his interest definitely piqued. His eyes bored into my very soul as they locked on mine, like a predator preparing to strike. "Where was the break-in?"

"His apartment."

"Apartment? I'm surprised whoever broke in didn't burn the joint down completely." He muttered a slur under his breath, and I didn't need to ask for clarification. His feelings were quite obvious. "I would've burned it down. Any chance I get to strike that man, I'll take it. But I'm not alone in feeling that way. There'd be a hundred volunteers lined up to take him out."

"Thankfully, the building didn't get burned down."

"Thankfully," he said, then followed it up with a brief chuckle. "So, what brings you down to my part of the world? Mr. Arrogant thinks it was me?"

"No, he hasn't mentioned your name."

"Someone did." He took another sip from his drink. "Otherwise you wouldn't be here."

"Yes, someone did, although not in the way you might assume."

"How so?"

"A woman he's been seeing. She told me that the only person Mark Costa has ever confided in her about was you."

That got him laughing again. This time, it was enough for the chuckle to turn into a long and guttural cough. When he got himself back under control, his face turned serious again.

"It's good to hear that I get under his skin. That prick is evil; you hear me? I doubt he could name enough people who like him to count one on each finger of one hand. He's a snake who feeds off misery. If he can make your life hell, he will. If there's one thing I take pride in, Mr. Investigator, it's ensuring I run my business in a way that would make my sweet old mother proud. I learned a long time ago that business doesn't have to be all lies and secrets. It can be conducted with a little bit of self-respect and some good old-fashioned hard work. I'm sure a man like you could understand that. You look like you have a bit of dignity about you."

"Yes, sir."

"So Mark Costa was robbed, and the cops can't solve it, even though he has a few of them in his back pocket. Whatever was taken must've been very valuable. Company secrets, perhaps?" He leaned in again, as if to reveal some deep, dark secret. "Let me tell you something. Mark Costa has crossed a lot of people in his time since taking the reins from Sergio. Lord knows why Sergio would ever hand them over in the first place. The man worked his butt off to get that company to where it was. I didn't like Sergio, but I respected him. Sergio was hard, brutal even, but he had honor. Mark Costa is a different breed. He's a spoiled little kid that took his father's name and trampled on it. You won't find anyone who'd be willing to have his back. He's been crossing the wrong people."

He leaned in closer. He had my attention, this time completely. He was about to give me something worthwhile. I held my breath and heard him out.

"Do you know who Lee Chan is?" he said.

The name rattled me, not because of personal dealings, but because it was a name that had graced every news channel at some time or another.

Wright could see I recognized the name. "The one and only. Mark Costa has been dealing with the Chinese Triads for the past few months, and word on the street is, he hasn't been keeping up his end of the deal."

The last thing I needed was to go looking for the

Chinese Mafia. The Triads weren't exactly known for their warm welcomes.

"How deeply is he involved?" I asked.

"About as deep as you can get. Simply doing a job for them here or there is one thing, but when you use their money? That's on a whole new level of climbing into bed with someone. Like I said, I'm surprised whoever it was that robbed him didn't burn his apartment to the ground. He certainly deserves it." He looked at his watch. "Listen, I'm expecting an important call any second. I'd love to sit here and chat about the end of Mark Costa, but I've got work to do."

"You've been very helpful, Mr. Wright," I offered, extending my hand.

"Call me Julian." He shook my hand and then looked me up and down. "You're a big guy—if you ever want a job in construction, give me a call. Might be hope to make an honest man out of you yet." He shot me a final wink, then returned to his laptop, forgetting about me and the rest of the irrelevant world in a heartbeat.

Once I was back in the truck, I phoned Casey on my cell. She picked up on the second ring, sounding as disappointed as I'd ever heard her.

"I got nothing interesting on Mindy, just some posts on social media about raving at a number of underground clubs," she said. "I hope you had better luck with your lead."

"I did, although I'm not sure it's anything I really wanted popping up." This caught her attention, and I heard papers shuffle in the background as she asked for more information.

"Bad news?"

"That depends on where it takes us," I began, firing up the truck and letting it rumble as I spoke. "Turns out Mark Costa has been bedding with Lee Chan's gang, so to speak. Wright said he's up to his neck in it and apparently holding out on some financial incentives."

"He's cheating the Triads?" She groaned at that, and I heard some more papers shuffling. She paused briefly, perhaps looking through her notes, before continuing. "Where to from here?"

"Think I'll have some Chinese for an early dinner," I said, trying to sound obvious. It wasn't how I imagined my evening playing out, but at that moment, I couldn't see any other options. If the Triads had a reason to rob our client, I needed to follow it up.

"You're going to check out the Triads? Jack, you can't. It's too dangerous." I felt the concern from her. "We have to give them a wide berth until we're absolutely sure they're involved. Let's not make any hasty decisions about going down that path."

"I'll be ok. I think it's time I paid him a visit." Lee Chan had crossed my desk once or twice in the past and meeting the man might pay off in the future.

"Jack, watch your step and watch your mouth," she said. "Because if you don't, that meal will be your last one ever."

CHAPTER 11

THE SUN had disappeared behind a layer of gray clouds by the time I had parked my truck. Any hint of warmth during the day had well and truly faded, with a damp chill hanging in the air. The smell of winter was still hanging around, and I wondered whether I should've grabbed something a little more substantial than just a t-shirt and leather jacket.

The weather should've been the furthest thing from my mind as I turned the engine off. Lee Chan had to be sitting front and center. He had to be my focus. I knew attempting to question him would be a huge gamble, but that's what the job called for.

I sat in my truck for an hour, several trains of thought running through my mind, ranging from the memorial with Casey to that first meeting with Mark Costa himself and how he'd approached me outside that little gathering. The comfort and silence of my truck cabin was perfect, providing just the right amount of freedom to let my mind wander. If Mark Costa was going to continue to occupy my mind, I needed to have the least number of distractions as possible.

I again wondered whether he'd attended the memorial simply to hire me or whether he was genuinely there to mourn the loss of an old friend. From what we'd found, he didn't have many friends, and there weren't a lot of people who spoke in his favor. If anything, the man was unlikely to go out of his way for anything unless it benefited him somehow.

And that's where it lay—the prospect of Mark Costa going out of his way for something that didn't benefit him. From where I was sitting, the only benefit for him attending was access to Casey. But why? There were plenty of private investigators in the book. It didn't take much effort to find a vast list of possibilities. He could even ask one of his many colleagues or staff, for that matter. Referrals came with somewhat of a guarantee of quality, and as far as I knew, no one from his circle even knew me. That was not counting Casey, and I didn't think she considered herself a part of his circle. So, why us?

I couldn't come to any definite conclusion. My best guess was that he didn't trust anyone else and perhaps also needed someone who came from as far away from his circle as possible. Why? Because of what was on the laptop. The footage had played a huge role in gaining the upper hand over his father, effectively blackmailing the man out of his own company. If anybody from within that circle found out about the blackmail, or the tool used, they might take it further.

He needed someone fresh, someone not related to anybody on his payroll, nor related to him in some way. A fresh person, a newcomer, someone who would take things a step at a time. And by getting someone fresh, he'd also be in a position to spoon-feed them the details of the case. He could effectively keep everything close to his chest and only release bits when he absolutely had to.

I let the thought slip from my mind as I turned my focus to the restaurant. The bright red letters of the 'Imperial Dragon' lit up in the big plate-glass window. A string of lanterns hung suspended along the front of the roofline, each shining in a different color. There were groups of people coming and going through the front doors, and from where I was sitting, I could see nothing more than a normal Chinese restaurant. To the untrained eye, it made for the perfect dinner destination.

But it was the hidden secrets that gave this particular restaurant its notoriety, known to cops, the media, and anybody in the game. The Imperial Dragon was the central hub for a criminal known as Lee Chan, also known as the head of a branch of the Chicago Triads. He was respected by many, a man who held honor in high regard, but behind the scenes, he was a ruthless businessman, renowned for cutthroat deals involving drugs, prostitution, and whatever ventures were worth the man's time. And he's not the most welcoming guy around.

After my meeting with Julian Wright, I'd found a bar and spent fifty minutes on my phone, searching the internet for anything relating to a possible Mark Costa/Lee Chan partnership. I knew there was something linking the pair, and I tried my best to see whether I could find that connection.

At first, I'd assumed that a property developer, one as high profile as Mark Costa, might've been selected by the gang to build them a new base of operations, perhaps a building in which to run their grand empire. But the more I dug, the more I realized that it wouldn't be as simple as that.

It took almost an hour of working my way through

idea after idea of possibilities before I realized I'd been searching in the wrong places. Chan hadn't employed Costa to build him anything. What I had found went much deeper than that.

One of Lee Chan's cousins, a man named Ye Ping, owned several factories on the outskirts of Shanghai. The merchandise he dealt in was building supplies, the kind that a property developer like Mark Costa could use every day of the year. By having Costa order his materials from the Shanghai firm, the Triads would simply add their own cargo to the order and collect upon delivery.

Whilst this information was readily available online, it called for a bit of reading between the lines, but it was that very type of reading which I dealt with in my business. Being a private investigator had taught me a lot about how people operated, and discovering the link between Lee Chan, Mark Costa, and Ye Ping, it made perfect sense. And now it was time to see whether I could find any proof of the deal.

I stepped out into the cool evening air. The parking lot was almost completely full, and I managed to mingle amongst several groups as they made their way inside at the same time. Once inside, it would just be a matter of time before I would strike gold.

The air hung heavy with the aromas associated with a Chinese restaurant. The smell of a deep fryer was intermingled with sharp spices, the kind that created some of my favorite flavors. The smells were so thick; I could almost taste them.

There was a small desk near the front door, complete with the typical golden cat, one paw busy waving to passing customers. I was held up temporarily with the other people in the foyer. The door into the main restaurant was hidden behind a divider, but I could hear the noise coming from the mix of voices beyond the door. I waited patiently as several greeters met with the guests ahead of me, and when it was my turn, I simply asked for a table for one.

I had no real plan at this point, other than simply gaining entrance into the establishment. I figured that once I was seated at a table, I could work my way through any number of possibilities, but I needed a way inside in order to make any of them viable.

At the edge of the room, I saw a man picking up takeout by the counter, and I had to look twice. It was the Russian security guard, Ivan Pushkin. That concerned me. What was his interest here? We made eye contact, and he held it for one long moment before he looked away.

"I'm sorry, Sir," a young man said, interrupting me before I could approach Ivan. The young man was well-groomed, with a clean American accent. "We have no availability this evening. All tables are booked."

"Could you take another look, please?" I asked, then held out my hand, a $20 neatly folded between my fingers. For a brief moment, I didn't think it would work. But money held power in its own right and it didn't matter where you were in the world. When someone offered you a financial reward for doing nothing more than your job, you simply held your hand out and took it.

"I'm sorry, Sir. Yes, you're right. We have one table that has just become available." He turned and gestured for me to follow. "Right this way, Sir."

I took one last look at Ivan Pushkin as he picked up a bag full of takeout, and then followed the young man behind the divider and through a small doorway that led down a narrow corridor, perhaps a dozen feet in length. As I stepped through into the main section of the restaurant, the smells increased, and I could see table after table loaded with all manner of culinary delights. My stomach growled in anticipation as I followed the waiter towards my own table.

I was led to a table for one, set against the side of a staircase that led up to another level. The waiter pulled out the chair for me to sit then handed me a single menu.

"Would you care for a drink before your meal, Sir?" I nodded.

"A beer, thanks."

"We have 'Tsingtao' beer. It's Chinese."

"If it tastes like beer, then that'll do."

"Yes, sir." He nodded and disappeared back into the crowd.

I looked around and found that the bottom level was where the majority of the customers sat, with maybe two dozen tables making up the main area. There were several booths running around the outside walls, each one filled with families, their tables loaded with multiple dishes.

The tables around me were lively with conversations, some between entire families, while others between couples. The voices rose and fell, with a hint of oriental music coming from random speakers I hadn't seen. Like many Chinese restaurants, there was a fish tank along one wall, filled with creatures that weren't just for decoration. Diners would walk up to it occasionally and point to one of the unfortunate occupants, while a waiter or waitress would carefully remove them from the tank and whisk them away to their final doom.

It was to the second level that I found my attention drawn. There were a number of tables up there, but it was just one I immediately noticed. Sitting at it were two men, with another two standing immediately behind them. I couldn't quite make out the seated men, but somehow, I knew that one of them was Lee Chan himself.

The man had a distinctive neck tattoo that I could just make out from where I sat, as well as one on the side of his bald head. His appearance looked as threatening as his reputation, and I knew I would be walking a fine line to try and get near him. But I also knew that my answers sat at the top of those stairs and that's where I needed to get to.

Once the waiter brought my beer, he asked for my order, and I opted for the Peking duck. It'd been one of my favorites for a long time and seemed an obvious choice. Once the waiter disappeared with my order, I returned my attention upstairs, sipping my drink and watching for anything of interest. Little did I know that it was a meal I would never get to finish.

I'd almost finished my beer when a voice spoke to me. It came from over my left shoulder. When I turned to see the two men standing there, I knew I had no choice but to comply.

"Mr. Chan would like to see you upstairs, Mr. Valentine." Not only did they know me by name, but they also knew my reason for being there. The first was confirmed; the second, a guess. I wondered whether Mark Costa had somehow managed to track me down and give me up, or whether my previous meeting with Julian Wright had something to do with it. "I suggest you move now because he doesn't enjoy being kept waiting."

I took their advice because these guys seemed anything but sociable.

CHAPTER 12

WITHOUT CAUSING a scene in the Chinese restaurant, I rose to my feet and followed one of the men as he led me towards the foot of the stairs, with the other man following close behind. We ascended to the second level as a trio, and once we reached the top, the first man broke away, leaving me to walk the rest of the way alone.

Lee Chan never looked up, continuing to watch the families enjoying their meals on the main floor beneath him. The second floor was a mezzanine style, open to the main floor, with only a hip-high railing to block Chan's view of the restaurant. His former table mate had disappeared, leaving Chan sitting alone with a bowl of soup in front of him. He was dressed in a fitted suit. He sat with a rigid posture. He moved slowly and with purpose. He presented himself as a leader, the ruthless king of his domain, governing those beneath him with poise.

The two men standing behind him remained in place, both watching me intently. I had no doubt that hidden beneath their suit jackets were the kinds of weapons that made quick work of nosy private investigators, and I wasn't about to test the theory.

"You must have impressed Julian somehow," Chan said, his voice sporting a hint of an accent. "He told me about you."

"I'm a popular guy." I wasn't going to bow to this guy. I needed to see whether he was every bit as ruthless as the rumors made him out to be. "People like to talk about me."

He turned to look at me, and it was the first time that I looked into his eyes. He had piercingly blue eyes. It actually gave me the shudders, only adding to his manipulative powers.

"Go ahead," he said, turning back to look at the people below. "Ask your questions."

"I'm not here for anything major. Just a few questions about a robbery that occurred at Mark Costa's apartment."

"I know it's not major. You wouldn't have made it inside if I considered it to be a major problem."

"Was it you that ordered the break-in of Costa's apartment?" I started with an easy one and he simply smiled before answering.

"Do I strike you as someone involved in simple robberies? Apartment robbery isn't something I consider worthy of my time."

"You didn't get one of your colleagues to drop by?" I knew I was fishing for all the wrong answers, but needed to press a further explanation out of him.

"Mark Costa has crossed me and if I wanted anything from him, I would be sure to get it from him directly. I'm not in the habit of sneaking around in the dark…" He turned back to me, as if to drum home his point. "…like some cheap, low-level private investigator."

That stung.

"But he's crossed you, that much I know. Julian filled me in on your dealings with Mark Costa."

"He has. And when the time is right, I'll go

looking for what he owes me. But for the time being, I have bigger fish to fry."

I don't know why, but for some reason, I knew Lee Chan was a careful criminal, a man not fazed by the little people like myself. He had a lot of the qualities I associated with Mark Costa, namely enjoying the notoriety. For a lot of criminals, that was part of the appeal. The power, the prestige, the infamy. He spoke without a care in the world. For all he knew, I could've been wearing a wire, with the cops waiting en-mass directly outside. And yet, none of it seemed to bother him.

"Will Mark Costa walk away from this with his arms and legs intact?" I asked. That seemed to push a button with him.

"Since when do you care about what happens to Mark Costa?" He seemed to know more than he let on and I wondered how much more I could get from him.

"Costa is paying my bills and I'd like to make sure that I'll still get paid."

"You need job security?" He laughed again. "Perhaps you should go home and mourn your wife, Mr. Valentine, and leave these sorts of things to the adults."

That caught me off guard and somehow winded me mentally for the moment. He saw my reaction and looked mighty pleased with himself. It was a revelation I hadn't counted on.

"Yes, we also do our homework. Now you can leave."

"So, I can count on Mr. Costa still being around for the next few weeks?" I paused, and then landed a heavy blow of my own. "Or will the next shipment be his final one?"

It was Chan's turn to look surprised. He turned and gazed at me, his eyes working me over, attempting to see inside my very soul. It appeared to me as if my hunch had in fact been closer to the truth than I suspected. A lot closer. His bodyguards shuffled forward, while Chan continued to stare.

"You're a brave man in a dirty world, Mr. Valentine. I respect that you've somehow managed to find out sensitive information, so I'll warn you once—it would serve you well to keep your mouth shut from now on. It is not difficult to make Private investigators disappear."

The threat came through crystal clear. Before I had a chance to respond, he turned back to the crowd, waved a hand towards me, and waited for his goons to escort me back down the stairs. Unsurprisingly, they didn't stop until I was back out in the parking lot.

I didn't ask for my order of Peking Duck. I imagine if I did, it would've been force-fed to me.

I walked back to my truck, realizing that I'd chosen to park in a dimly lit area. That wasn't a bright idea. As I approached my truck, I fumbled for the keys and dropped them. I bent down to retrieve them, and as I did, pain exploded in my right temple, temporarily turning night into a brilliant display of stars.

"Stay out of our business, rent-a-cop," a voice heckled as a boot slammed into my stomach. The wind was knocked out of me, and my legs buckled. I gasped for air and would've ended up on the ground if it wasn't for the nearby fence post.

As a shadow came flying towards me, I turned and

sprang forward, leading with my right fist. The straight right caught the short assailant on the jaw and his intended attack fell short.

There was a scream near me, and I ducked as something whistled across the top of my head. I imagined a razor-sharp blade of some sort and thrust my elbow up to the side. I must've found just the right spot, because the short sharp gasp that sailed out from the darkness reminded me of every man's worst pain.

Before I had a chance to stand and finish the fight, another voice came from somewhere behind me, this one with a lot more control than the previous two.

"Enough."

I stood and looked at the third bodyguard. He gripped a handgun held in front of him, although not aimed at me. The other two men half-crawled back towards him, one of them carefully holding his package in one hand as he walked.

"It would be in your best interest to stay out of our business, Mr. Valentine."

Despite coming out of the fight in better shape, the message was loud and clear, and I didn't need a second lesson. If I knew these people, and I think I'm a pretty good judge of character, there'd be no further lessons. The next time these people came calling, it would be to end me.

The three of them disappeared back into the darkness, and I stood my ground for a few moments. Once I couldn't see any more movements around me, I continued to my truck. Their attack proved my investigative assumptions were still in tiptop condition.

I jumped in my truck and decided to head back to

the office instead of home. I had a better computer there, as well as a couch that I had always found more comfortable than my bed at home. I needed to get deeper into the types of dealings Mark Costa had been getting himself involved in while the day's events were still fresh in my head.

I checked the rear-view mirror as I drove to the office, checking for any tails. I didn't see anyone on the drive. There was a multi-level parking lot behind my office building, with several vehicles already parked for the night. That wasn't unusual, considering there was a small apartment complex next door. I parked, checked my surroundings, and then entered the office.

I didn't relax again until I was safely inside the office. There wasn't any doubt in my mind that I was safe, but the adrenalin was still raging.

Once I was sitting behind a locked door with an open bottle of Mr. Jack Daniels for company, I started to breathe a little easier. I wondered whether I had done the right thing by approaching the Chinese restaurant, or instead, awoken an unnecessary inconvenience that could essentially silence the lot of us without a second thought.

Only time would tell.

CHAPTER 13

IT WASN'T the first time I'd slept at the office, and I knew that it certainly wouldn't be the last. The one benefit, other than the comfy couch, was knowing Casey would be in first thing, no doubt with fresh coffee in her hand. I was already sitting up as she came through the door, pausing long enough to take her sunglasses off and just stare at me.

"Did we spend the night at the office? Certainly devoted." She didn't see the scratch on the side of my face until she was handing me the cup of coffee, then didn't hold back with her 'I told you so' speech. "Geez, Jack. What happened?"

"I had an assumption confirmed," I whispered, taking the lid off the cup and letting the warmth of my first sip run down my throat.

"An assumption?" She went into the small kitchenette, and I heard the faucet turn on. A moment later, she returned and began to dab at my temple where the blood I failed to notice had dried into an ugly patch. "What sort of assumption?"

"It probably looks worse than it is. I just got jumped, that's all."

"Jumped? By how many? Five guys?"

"The burger restaurant didn't attack me," I joked. "It was just three."

"Oh, just three. Well, that's ok then." She wasn't

happy and I felt foolish trying to make light of the situation. I'd been lucky to come out of the ambush with just a small wound and a bruised ego. Others had likely ended up in the hospital for less.

"You're angry. I'm sorry, Casey."

"Yeah, well, you should be. You could've been killed."

"You're right." It was pointless to deny it, so I just sat there and took my medicine.

When she was done, Casey went and sat at the table, dropped her handbag on top, and just stared. The tension in the air wasn't something new to me, with her protective instinct switched to maximum. I couldn't blame her. If I'd listened to her, I might've saved the both of us from a lot more grief than we needed right then.

"So?" she asked, her patience wearing thin. "Do I need to ask for the details?"

She didn't, and as we took time drinking our morning coffee, I filled her in on the events from the previous evening. I told her about Lee Chan, about my assumptions regarding Mark Costa's involvement in some of their activities, and how I had baited the man. I told her that I saw Ivan Pushkin, the Russian security guard at the restaurant, picking up takeout. And then I told her how three guys jumped me, and warned me to stay out of their business. When I finally finished, silence descended over us once more as she worked the conversation over in her mind. When she spoke again, it was more of the same.

"You don't mind playing with fire, do you, Jack? I mean to throw something like that out there? Did you think Lee Chan was just going to pat you on the back for uncovering their little activities?" She looked past me and out through the window. "Will I need to start watching my back now?"

"No, of course not. It's done with."

"How can you be sure?"

"Because Lee Chan has got a lot more on his plate than little old me."

She wasn't impressed and didn't mind letting me know. "I hope you're right. Because if they come looking, I'm telling you now, I'll be out of here. They're not the people I want to mess with. People don't get a second chance with these guys."

I nodded, and she smiled, shaking her head at me. Then I knew the seriousness of the situation had passed. She'd forgiven me without saying the words, and we had effectively moved on.

"Looks like we have to check further into Ivan Pushkin," I said, taking another sip. The coffee was good, hot, and strong enough to strip paint. Exactly how I enjoyed it. "He could be our middleman. His appearance at the restaurant last night might've moved him into first place. The other person with access to the apartment is Lauren Taylor, the cleaner. They could all be in on this together."

"I'll see what else I can find. I'll check and see if there's any link between Ivan, Mindy, Lauren, or the Triads." Casey turned on her computer. "I've got a new facial recognition program that I've been eager to run, so it looks like Ivan will be the first volunteer."

"Well, I'm sure he's not 'Russian' to be part of the program."

"Enough of the 'rushing' jokes," Casey rolled her eyes. "If you make another one of those jokes, I'm going to call Lee Chan personally and ask him to punch you."

While Casey began the search on her new program, I went to my office, retrieved the spare shirt I always kept in the small bathroom and changed, rolling on some deodorant during the process. Once I had reduced the offensive smell surrounding me and made myself a little more presentable, I returned back into the office where Casey was researching our new target.

"It looks like he's worked for Sergio Costa before," Casey said. "Four years ago, when he first moved to America, he worked for the 'Apex' restaurant as a kitchen hand, before he became a security guard. His photo was picked up by the facial recognition program I ran because his photo was posted on the restaurant's Facebook page."

"How'd you find that?"

"It's the new program," she tapped her computer screen. "I upload a number of photos into the program, and then it scans the internet for any possible match. The system will present numerous options, and I have to define the parameters for the photo. I've kept the date range limited to five years, as people's facial features can change over time. It's best to upload an early photo of the suspect and then a current photo. The system will then work out the differences in-between." Casey clicked her fingers. "And within fifteen minutes, I have every photo of Ivan Pushkin that's available on the internet."

"What else have you got?"

"A couple of photos where he's in the background of other people's shots," she paused for dramatic effect, "And get this—I have a few photos of him attending some underground raves."

"Any link to Mindy?"

"None yet, but I'll check if Mindy posted photos of the same raves."

"You're very good at this, Casey," I said. "That would've taken me years to find out the old way."

"It's promising," Casey said. "But there are no known links to the Chinese Triad."

"Either way, it sounds like it's time to have a more intimate chat." I grabbed my jacket off the hook. "And it might be quite revealing."

CHAPTER 14

WE'D ONLY driven a few miles before my phone rang. It was Mark Costa again. I let the call go to voicemail and then played it back on speaker-phone once he'd finished.

"I need that laptop, Jack. I'm getting impatient." His tone was angry. "I need it back and I need it now." He ended the call without so much as even a goodbye.

I looked at Casey in the passenger seat, and she didn't say anything. She could feel the pressure from where she sat.

"Our Russian also works at an upmarket bar in Northbrook as a bouncer," Casey read something off her phone. "A second security guard job, which, I might add, is only a stone's throw from Sergio Costa's restaurant."

"He works all the way up there?"

"It looks like just on Saturday nights," Casey continued reading. "Once a week, according to the data that I've got. Works at the apartment building during the week, and picks up extra shifts at the bar over the weekend. Works at the Five-Pillar Monday to Friday, and then picks up a shift Saturday night."

I tapped my thumb on the steering wheel as we drove towards the Five-Pillar apartment building, the thoughts running through my head. Despite a long history of conflict between our countries, I liked Russians—most of them I'd worked with were no-nonsense, hardworking, and had extreme tolerance for the cold. They were also some of the most emotionless people I knew. I never had to worry about one of them breaking down in tears and complaining about their feelings.

We parked in an underground lot close by and walked towards the parking garage for the Five-Pillar building. Walking down the ramp, we came to a large metal gate. I walked over to the side, pressed the call button, and then looked up at the camera. When I didn't hear any movement from inside the gates, I turned to Casey.

"It looks like he's not 'Russian' to help us out."

"Oh. Can you please stop it? I swear if you make that joke one more time, I'm going to walk out of here."

I laughed and then pushed the button again and waved. This time, I heard the door to the security office open and the heavy footsteps of a man approaching.

The metal door swung open, and the security guard stared at us. Again, there wasn't so much as a hello.

"Ivan Pushkin." I greeted him. "We'd like to have a chat."

He stared at me. There was no life, no fire, and no anger behind his eyes.

"Can we come into your office and chat in a quieter environment?" Casey asked in a softer tone.

"No." His response was blunt, and he didn't elaborate further.

"Why not?"

"We are busy monitoring the building. We do not have time to play games with investigators. If you wish to talk further, contact the police department. I've told them everything I know."

"We would like to know why you were at the Imperial Dragon last night," I said. "I saw you there."

"I was there for food." Again, his response was blunt, but this time he continued. "To eat."

Despite the added information, he wasn't exactly forthcoming.

"We know that you've worked for Sergio Costa in the past at the Apex restaurant," I hit him with the information. "And we also know that Sergio is trying to muscle his way in on his son's business. His son has an apartment in the building where you work security. That's a big coincidence."

Again, he didn't respond. He continued to stare at me. I didn't flinch and nor did he. While I liked that the Russians were good at hiding their feelings, it was hard to read them. I couldn't tell if he was just being cold, or he was hiding something.

"Could you please tell us where you were on the 5th of May, the night of the robbery?" Casey's voice was soft, in contrast to my harshness. "We'd like to cross you off the list."

"What night was it?"

"A Thursday night."

"I worked and then I went home. I was at home during the night."

"Can anyone verify that?"

"No."

"Is there something that could prove you were home? Perhaps some video footage or your phone's location?"

"No."

"Did anyone see you leave work that night?" Casey continued.

"Mindy—" He stopped halfway through saying the name, but we heard him loud and clear.

"Mindy Fox?" Casey questioned. "Mark Costa's friend? Did she see you before you left work that day?"

"You're not the police. I don't have to answer your questions." His jaw clenched this time. He'd had very few emotional reactions in our few interactions, but this was a clear sign that he was getting angry and impatient. "It is time for you to go."

"Hold up," I said. "We haven't finished talking to you yet."

"I have finished talking to you."

He went to shut the door, but I stuck my foot against the bottom of it, which stopped him from closing it. He looked at me, then looked at my foot, and then back to stare at my eyes. We held the stare for a few moments, and when I was sure that he understood that we weren't giving up on the lead, I removed my foot.

He held the door for a moment longer, and then closed it, complete with the sound of two locks clicking behind it. Casey raised her eyebrows as she looked at me. I nodded to confirm her suspicions.

We didn't say another word until we were back in the truck, when Casey broke the silence.

"Mindy Fox?" She asked. "You think they could be dating?"

"It sounds like those two know each other quite well," I replied. "And she might be able to give us some more answers."

CHAPTER 15

WE PULLED up to the nearest strip mall. Casey headed in to grab food while I jumped on the laptop in the truck and began looking at some of Ivan Pushkin's previous dealings. I had a hunch that he knew a lot more about the robbery than he was letting on, but I wasn't sure who he was connected to. Sergio Costa? Possibly. Mindy Fox? Maybe. The Triads? Could be. This was an inside job, and Ivan Pushkin fit the profile of the inside man. Did he have a motive for stealing the laptop himself? We didn't know, but it made sense that his services were available to the top buyer. But who was the buyer?

Sergio Costa was my best bet. He knew what was on the laptop. He knew of the footage. And he was the only one who could benefit from getting ahold of the laptop's contents, and with the apartment not completely destroyed, it made sense. That would rule out the Chinese Triad connection, although I couldn't completely discount them.

No, to me, this robbery had a personal feel to it. It had to be.

Casey returned with a couple of meatball sandwiches for me and a Vietnamese pork roll for herself. We sat on the back gate of the truck, watching the world go by in the parking lot. Casey passed across a coke, and I downed almost half a bottle on my first swig. I hadn't paid attention to just how thirsty I was and once I finished the first of the meatball sandwiches, I realized my hunger wasn't far behind. We ate while making a little small talk and Casey complained how one of her friends is always wearing Crocs to various functions and how he's always fashionably late.

"If you arrive fashionably late in Crocs, you're just late," I said.

Casey began to snort with laughter, more than the quote deserved, and then she burst into a frightening coughing fit. I jumped up to help her, but she held a hand up, and her face contorted into a weird strain of angst. It was only when the color returned to her cheeks that she sat up properly and spoke.

"Well, that wasn't pleasant."

"Thought I was going to have to do the Heimlich maneuver," I said.

She began to laugh again, and it reminded me of a time when Claire had choked on some shrimp during a trip through Maine. That time I actually did need to do the Heimlich maneuver, and it became somewhat of a joke between us. The day a shrimp brought us closer together.

Once Casey and I finished our food, our attention turned back to the case, deciding it might be a good time to return to the intended owner of the bracelet and Ivan's possible girlfriend.

"Stakeout her apartment?" Casey asked.

I hadn't really spent too much time considering the options, thinking more about simply talking to her again. But once Casey mentioned it, perhaps assuming that's what my intention had been, I figured it would probably serve us a little better.

"It'll tell us if Ivan is coming and going."

We decided it was the right move and drove towards the Roseland neighborhood on the south side of the city.

"There are two possibilities with the bracelet we found," I stated as we drove along the Chicago Skyway part of the I-90, raised above the passing neighborhoods on Chicago's South Side. "One, Mark Costa dropped it before he had the chance to give it to her, or…"

"Mindy dropped it while in that room," Casey finished the sentence. "Does she have another excuse to be in that room? What business would she have near the desk, if any at all? You saw what was in there. A desk, a cupboard, and a safe. And apart from that, nothing but boxes that contained files from his job. Not really the kind of thing a girlfriend would want to go through."

"And she's not really a girlfriend, either."

As we got closer to Mindy's address, which we'd found after a quick google search, Casey began to call out directions, a left here, right there, and a second right here. Eventually, we ended up on a road lined with the kinds of buildings where happy families were a rarity, if they existed in the area at all. The misery from within the structures seemed to bleed outwards. Mindy's apartment building was one of the better-looking ones, although it too appeared to have seen its last good day during the Kennedy years. Several windows looked broken, with skimpy sheets of plywood doing their best to keep the weather out.

There weren't many other cars parked on the street, and Casey suggested I hang back a little, a consideration I had already agreed to in my mind.

Once parked behind an old bus that looked abandoned and possibly lived in, I killed the engine and sat back to wait things out.

"Should we go in and have a look around?" Casey asked after a few minutes, and I shook my head.

"Not yet. Better to sit things out for a bit." After another minute, I added, "Never know what these stakeouts can produce sometimes."

Several people passed the truck, some walking dogs, others carrying grocery bags. Cars didn't seem to be a common possession in this neck of the woods, and given the number of cars we'd passed sitting on bricks, I doubt even my truck would have lasted a night if left unattended.

A gang of five youths walked past, saw us sitting in the truck, and began to taunt us with things like, "Five-oh sittin' on a bust." We ignored them, and when we didn't react the way they'd hoped, they moved on up the street, but not before sending a wolf whistle to a girl walking the other way. Thankfully, none of them laid a hand on her, which prevented me from being forced to intervene, which was fortunate since we didn't know whether Mindy was home and I didn't need to risk her spotting us.

It didn't take much longer before a development took place. It was Casey that spotted our target, and when I looked up, I saw Mindy standing at the top of the steps leading into her building. She was coming out, dressed in jeans and a gray sweatshirt with the hood on. She turned left and made her way to a corner store that sat half a block back.

We sat and waited for the girl to reappear. As we did, Casey's phone pinged.

She read the message while I kept an eye on the

entrance to the store.

"Interesting," she said. "A source of mine has passed on some news about Sergio Costa. Apparently, he's rented a storage locker ten minutes' drive from his son's apartment."

"That is interesting," I replied. I turned to look at Casey, the development more than intriguing to me. "Does he have any other businesses nearby? Why would he rent something so close?" I asked, positive there would be better choices in the neighborhoods around his own area of the city.

"I'm not sure yet. But something tells me it's not just a coincidence," Casey said. "My contact knows Sergio Costa and has heard the rumor through the grapevine. I put out the feelers yesterday to see if anyone knows anything unusual about him, and it looks like someone has come through."

"Maybe Sergio is thinking of taking over the helm again. Maybe he wants something close by where he can keep an inventory of what Mark is holding."

"Or maybe there's something worthwhile stored in there?"

"A lot of maybes." I turned back towards the end of the street, just in time to watch Mindy come out of the store and return in the direction of her apartment building. Shortly after, she disappeared back inside.

"Now what?" Casey asked a little impatiently. At the apartment, a man was climbing the stairs to the front door.

"Now we wait a little longer." Patience was definitely not one of Casey's virtues. "At least we know she's inside."

"Is that…" Casey leaned forward to get a closer look at the man walking up the steps to the apartment building. "Ivan Pushkin?"

I squinted. "You're right. It is. He must be on a break from the security office," I said, gripping the steering wheel a little tighter. "Now, we wait until they exit."

"Do you think he came here to warn her about what he said to us at the gate? He might be worried that he dropped Mindy into the mess?"

I agreed that it made sense and kept my eyes on the building. Fifteen minutes later, Ivan reemerged with Mindy beside him, her face anything but happy.

"Are they fighting?" Casey wound down her window. "I can hear them."

I nodded, watching as the pair exchanged verbal insults, Mindy pointing a finger into Ivan's face. He pushed it away, and when Mindy went to slap him, he grabbed her wrist and returned with a slap of his own. Physical altercations between two men were something I could handle. Between women, not so much. But when a man chooses to get physical with a woman? That's where I draw the line.

I'd seen enough and stepped out of the truck. Casey followed suit, but before we'd even reached the middle of the road, Ivan got into his sedan. He drove away without even looking back at us. I don't think he saw us. Mindy watched him disappear around the corner before turning back and spotting us.

"Mindy, we—" was all I got out before she turned and ran, this time ducking down a small alley beside the next building. She moved as fast as a jackrabbit, darting between two people on her way through. Casey was about to give chase, but I held out my hand and stopped her.

"No, wait. This isn't the right time."

"Did you see her eyes? I could have sworn she was high on something."

"She was," I agreed. "And if she doesn't want to talk to us, chasing her down won't help."

"Apartment?" Casey pointed to the building. "There's no one home."

"We could check if the door is open," I said. "And we might even stumble across a missing laptop."

As we walked up the steps to the apartment building, one of the other residents was waiting in the small entrance, next to the mailboxes. He was an older man, with the look of a community-watch type. He stood at the end of the hallway when we walked through. He asked if he could help us, but we didn't respond.

Casey and I had no choice but to walk out of the building. Our chance to check Mindy's apartment wouldn't happen now. We returned to the truck, hopped in, and drove back around the neighborhood for ten minutes, looking for Mindy. When we didn't spot her, we drove back to the office. It'd been a worthwhile trip, and we were getting close. If our progress continued the way it had been, we stood a chance of cracking the case before the following day was out.

Or so we thought.

CHAPTER 16

I DROPPED Casey back at the office to continue to dig around Mindy Fox's past and see if she could establish a motive to steal the laptop. We were close, but we needed a motive. It was all that was missing— what was her motive, and who was she working for? Was it worthwhile just getting the laptop back without the information about who they took it for? And did she still have the laptop in her apartment, or had she sold it to the highest bidder? It made no sense that she took it as part of the money heist—if it was just the money she was after, she would've left the laptop behind. Who would steal a five-year-old laptop without a motive?

My curiosity was getting the better of me, and there were questions about what Casey had shared earlier. The storage unit rented by Sergio Costa was just a couple of neighborhoods back from Mark Costa's home and a long way from Sergio's restaurant. The only sense I could make of it was if Sergio Costa did in fact intend to retake possession of the laptop and store it there. And the timeline had me question his intention as well. He'd rented the unit the same day we were hired. If it wasn't for the laptop, what business did he have there?

I still had the thoughts running through my mind when I drove out to meet Detective Troy Williams.

We met at a bar near off Michigan Ave., only a stone's throw from the Five-Pillar apartment building. Troy was an old friend who came through for me numerous times. He was a wealth of information, always with his finger on the pulse. As I drove to the bar, memories of Troy and I played out in my mind. He'd been there for me after my wife Claire died, attending the funeral and checking in on me from time to time. If there was one thing I knew about true friends, it was that those who showed up without an invite or reason would always be the ones most welcome. And Troy did a little of both.

Troy had set up some counseling sessions with a therapist during some of my darker days after the shooting. Although hesitant at first, I eventually gave in and found them to be quite helpful. Troy could be quite persuasive when he wanted to be. Eventually, however, even they couldn't help when grief really took hold. I figured they'd served their purpose as much as possible and pulled the pin on the rest. Part of me has always believed that Troy's actions during those first few months after the tragedy probably saved my life to some degree. Grief has a way of coming out. Way too many obstacles sit on the road to recovering from personal tragedy, and Troy had managed to save me from most of them.

The drive to the bar had its own drama, with a taxi almost colliding with me as it ran a stop sign. After the standard honk and giving him the finger out the window, the driver decided to slow down and engage in a little road rage. The ensuing verbal exchange at the next set of traffic lights did little to calm the adrenalin coursing through my body. But once he squealed his way around the corner and disappeared from view, I knew he was out of my life for good. When I walked into the bar, I was still edgy about the interaction I'd had on the road.

"Troy," I greeted him with a handshake and grabbed the stool next to his. "Looking good. I'm almost embarrassed I didn't get dressed up for the occasion."

He was dressed in a flashy suit, pinstripe, and outshone me in every way. His black hair was slicked back, and he was wearing a healthy dose of cologne.

"Another day in court," he groaned. "Don't think I dressed up to meet you."

"I'm offended," I joked. "I'm not worthy of getting dressed up for?"

"I love a good dress up party, but not for you." He smiled. "Last week, I saw a man walking down the road with a small woman on his back. I asked him where he was going, and he replied that he was going to a fancy-dress party as a tortoise. 'Then who's the woman on your back?' I asked. He pointed to her and said, 'That's Michelle.'"

I laughed heartily. He could always deliver a good joke.

After a few more minutes of idle chatter, Troy reached into his shirt pocket and pulled out an envelope, holding it out for me. He'd always been someone I could rely on, regardless of the request.

"I spoke to the detectives on this one," he said in a low tone. "They weren't fans of Mark Costa. He was quite rude to them, so there's not much hope of recovering the stolen cash. Things like this happen all the time, and I mean, who leaves $50K sitting around their apartment? No real leads and no real desire from the investigating cops to nail anyone for it."

I nodded my appreciation. "Anything useful at all?" I asked, knowing he would have scanned it himself ahead of time, if only to be able to give me some helpful advice. He considered before answering.

"They said it was definitely an inside job. Probably no surprise there. I'm sure you would've worked that one out. They had two main suspects—the cleaner, Lauren Taylor, and the security guard, Ivan Pushkin. They dismissed them both, however. They thought that Ivan Pushkin was the prime suspect."

"That was my thought as well. Their reasoning?"

"The building has an extensive security system, with some apartments containing internal cameras as well. Then there's the alarm system, the fact that it's the best money can buy, and it's being monitored. Both the alarm system and the cameras had been switched off moments before the break-in. And it turns out you can only access those servers from inside the building. The monitoring is in-house," he said. "And there's been issues with this security group before in separate buildings. They keep winning these big contracts to monitor apartment buildings, but the rumor is that they're connected to the criminal gangs and often sell out their clients."

"The question is, who were the insiders working for?"

"I take it this is more than about the cash then," Troy raised his eyebrows. "Something else was taken, wasn't it? Something that Mark Costa failed to disclose to the police?"

I nodded.

"Don't you just love a good mystery?" Troy swigged the rest of his beer, set his glass down, and ordered another. I joined him, and before long, we'd downed several more.

The conversation turned away from the case, and onto our own lives.

It was good to catch up with an old friend, almost therapeutic. We caught up on our current lives, relived our past, and shared all the best jokes we knew. The conversation see-sawed between old times and new, revisiting some of the war stories we had been telling each other for decades, embellishing them a little further each time. The drinks flowed as well as the conversation, and soon, I'd forgotten the purpose for my visit.

It wasn't long before we ordered wings, enough for the entire bar to feast on, if we'd been in a sharing kind of mood. The platter sat between us, and we didn't pause until there was a neat pile of bones in the center.

I excused myself and headed for the men's room, needing to take care of my sticky fingers and fast-filling bladder. One definitely took priority over the other.

I barely made it to the door when a new surprise presented itself—Ivan Pushkin and Mindy Fox were sitting in the corner of the bar.

CHAPTER 17

THE LAST place I expected to find Mindy Fox and Ivan Pushkin was the very bar where I'd met Troy, and yet as I headed for the men's room, that's who I spotted, sitting at a table near the back, hunched over their drinks. They weren't talking. I looked at my watch—five-past-six. Ivan would've finished work and met Mindy for a drink afterward, perhaps to discuss my presence near her apartment earlier that day.

If I hadn't gotten up at that moment, I might've missed them completely because as I watched, she rose to her feet, grabbed his hand, and they headed for the door. They hadn't seen me.

I looked over at Troy, whose attention had been drawn to the ballgame playing out on the television hanging behind the bar. He seemed content and would probably not notice my absence for a while, time which I hoped would be sufficient to get a few questions answered that had been fermenting in my mind. I say fermenting, because they were certainly beginning to feel old. I needed answers.

I followed the couple out the front door to the dim parking lot as the time ticked past 6pm. A light drizzle had begun to blanket the neighborhood, adding to the air of cloak and dagger. I didn't want to lose them and jogged to one of the exits. The parking lot had two, and I gave myself a 50/50 chance of getting it right.

My hunch paid off. I reached the road and spotted them walking into an alley a little further down the street. I jogged to the end of the alley, eager to keep an eye on them.

I was moving faster than I'd initially planned. It wasn't a smart move, and I rounded the corner much too fast. Experience should've told me to be more aware of my surroundings. But the alcohol had dulled my senses a lot more than I'd realized, and when I rounded the corner, Ivan threw a punch to my stomach, sending me to the ground.

"What do you want?" Ivan screamed down at me as I began to recover, more stunned than anything else. "Stop following us."

They both stood over me, and for a second, I expected a kick to the face. I wasn't going to give Ivan that chance. As I went to stand, Ivan swung his foot. I grabbed his ankle, and thrust my shoulder into his stomach. He went down quicker than I expected. He hit his head on the concrete as he went down, and stayed flat on his back.

Now, it was my turn to stand over him.

Fists clenched, ready to brawl, I stared at him. His eyes looked dazed from the fall.

"Stop it." Mindy stood back from me, arms folded across her chest. "What do you want? Why are you following us?"

"I want to know who asked you to steal the laptop."

"What laptop?" she snapped back. "From Mark Costa's place? The cops have already cleared us of any involvement."

"They already cleared us," Ivan repeated, beginning to sit up, rubbing the back of his head. "We don't have to answer to you."

"The police have cleared you." I stepped closer to Ivan, towering over him. "But I haven't."

"We didn't steal anything from his place," Mindy said. "It wasn't us."

"I need answers, and you'd better start talking," I said, as I turned my attention to Mindy. "The fact that you're dating both the security guard of the building and Mark Costa makes you a suspect. You hadn't mentioned that before."

"I didn't mention it because I didn't want Mark to find out." She stole a glance at Ivan. "Mark might've cut me off if he knew."

"What she does with him is purely for the money, nothing more," Ivan grunted. "The guy pays well, and that's as far as it goes."

"What do you need the laptop for?" I said, staring at Mindy, who had now stepped behind Ivan. "Are you somehow trying to blackmail Mark Costa? Either for cash or something else?"

"I don't have the laptop," she said. "I never did. I didn't steal anything from his place."

"If you took the money, that's fine," I said. "We don't care about the fifty-thousand in cash that was taken from the safe. All we care about is the laptop. If you admit it now, I won't even tell Mark Costa where we found the laptop. We can forget about the cash that was stolen from the safe. All I need is that laptop."

"Aren't you listening? She said that she didn't steal anything." Ivan rubbed the back of his head again.

"She wasn't involved in the burglary."

"I'm coming for you." I leaned down and brought my face close to Ivan's. "And when I find the evidence that you're involved, I'm going to bring the whole house down on top of you. Mark Costa won't be happy that you've crossed him."

Ivan held my stare for a long moment, before Mindy put her arms under his armpits and began to help him up. He stood slowly, and there was blood on the back of his head. Mindy checked the blood and then grabbed his hand and began to walk away. Soon, they disappeared into the shadows of the alley, leaving me standing at the end.

I watched them walk away, feeling the truth was only getting closer.

CHAPTER 18

MY HEAD didn't feel the best the next morning, and I put it down to a combination of the drink, taking a punch to the stomach, and failing to close my curtains before hitting the hay. By the time my eyes finally opened, the sun was blazing in through the window, and I could feel the resulting pounding in my skull.

There'd also been a dream. A bad one. I know that Claire was in it, and she was in trouble. Something was trying to take her, and she kept calling for me to come and help, only I couldn't. No matter how hard I tried to reach her, something kept dragging me back. Her scream was the last thing to pound through my head as I woke.

The phone rang, and once I managed to thumb the answer call button, Casey asked whether I was turning up for work. I looked at my watch and saw that it was five-past-nine.

"Sorry, kiddo. Didn't get in till late."

"Catch-ups have a tendency to do that to a person. Want me to drop by?"

I thought about it and quickly decided against it. "No, I need some fresh air, and it looks like a nice morning. Let's meet for a coffee at Roosevelt Park."

It was a small park near the office, one I hadn't been to in quite a while. It was a place where I tried to have lunch at least once a week, to get my vitamin D levels up, but it never quite took hold. Work, life, and commitments always had a way of stopping my plans.

"Sure thing, Jack. I'll grab you an extra-large coffee and a muffin, and I'll see you there at ten."

She knew the way to my heart.

I thanked her, hung up, and headed for the shower. The first thing, and the best thing, for my head was a cold dunking, and despite the initial shock, it felt amazing, my head thanking me not long after I climbed out. The rush of blood that came after the initial shock was almost euphoric.

Judging the day by the cold blasting through the bedroom window, I opted for a leather jacket and jeans, heading out of my place before 9:30. It didn't take long to make my way to the park, and I found Casey already sitting at one of the picnic tables, the coffee and muffin laid out on the table like a sacrificial offering.

I touched her on the shoulder and thanked her for being so good to me. I needed her to know that I appreciated it. Small gestures had a way of leaving big impressions. I took a sip of coffee, enjoyed it a little too much, and took another large gulp. In the cold air, it felt good, tasted better, and would shortly have an effect I considered the best.

We sat in silence, not because of a lack of words, but because the day was clear, the breeze felt refreshing, and the birds were singing in the trees above us. It was holistic and meditative sitting in that park, and words would not add value to the moment. It was only when we both finished the food that we spoke again, Casey asking me how the previous night went. I held up one hand and showed her my scraped palm, the grin on my face saying the rest.

"Again?" She rolled her eyes and shook her head. "Another five guys?"

"Not quite." I felt a little absurd and tried to defend myself before she ran away with the wrong idea. "I got surprised by Mindy Fox and her boyfriend, Ivan Pushkin."

"What?" She looked surprised at that, almost confused. "Mindy and Ivan? Where did you find them? I thought you were meeting up with Troy Williams?"

"I did, but during the night, I spotted Mindy and Ivan at the bar and, well, one thing led to another."

"One thing led to another?"

"It wasn't as if I jumped them."

"Go on. Tell me what happened."

"There's not much to explain. I was at the bar, having a drink and a laugh, when I saw Mindy holding Ivan's hand as she led him out of the place. I followed them, and they disappeared into an alley. I jogged to catch up, and Ivan sucker-punched me to the stomach. He went to kick me, but I threw him to the ground. It was quite the laugh," I smiled as I explained the exchange with Mindy and her man. Casey listened, although I wasn't sure she saw the humorous side of the exchange the way I did. "They denied ever having the laptop, or any knowledge of it."

"So the question remains—where is the laptop now," she paused. "And who took it in the first place?"

"Which is what we've been paid to find out," I thought back to how Mindy reacted when I threw the question at her. If there had been any hint of deception, I know I would've picked up on it. I hadn't. "And as much as I like Mindy and Ivan as the prime suspects, I have my doubts."

"Everything points to them," Casey continued. "If Sergio Costa had gone anywhere near the apartment, the cameras would've picked him up. There's just too much to overcome in that building. Even with all the alarms and cameras conveniently switched off, there's no getting around the staff and they couldn't all have been paid off. Perhaps Ivan was acting alone, and Mindy knows nothing about it? Maybe she spilled the inside scoop about the location of the laptop, and Ivan went in to get it. It's not the first time security would've been paid to look the other way. And think about it, it's a little too perfect for it to have been anyone else. And you know what they say—the logical conclusion, after everything else has been ruled out, no matter how unlikely, is normally the answer. They had access to the apartment and could've been there that day. So, do we just break down the door and ransack her apartment?"

Casey was both sincere and adamant, and for a moment, I wondered whether she was right. Maybe she had a point, and I was just too used to focusing on the things I understood the most. I needed to follow the facts and nothing more.

"I hear what you're saying, but there's one thing that doesn't fit with them."

"What's that?" She sipped her drink. "Everything fits in my book."

"If Mindy or Ivan were working for Sergio, my gut says that Sergio would've done something about it already. It's been over a week, and he hasn't made a move. If he had the laptop, Mark Costa would no longer be in charge of the business. Sergio Costa is not the type of man that sits around and waits. If he had it, he'd be charging back into the business like a bull in Pamplona."

"Pamplona?"

"In Spain. It's where they hold the running of the bulls. I did it one year when I was young. It was a great rush not to get impaled by an angry bull. That's how I think Sergio would react the second he had the laptop—he'd be charging back into that business and knocking down everyone in his way."

"Maybe," she conceded. "I can see that. It's been a week, and nothing's happened, and Sergio Costa doesn't seem like a man who likes to wait."

I scrunched up my trash, reached for Casey's, and walked it to the trashcan.

"Let's walk," I suggested, and she nodded, grabbing her drink and following me back towards the path. After a few yards, Casey surprised me with a question.

"Can I ask you something? Something personal?"

I nodded, unsure of where this might lead.

"Do you enjoy our work?" she asked, looking forward.

It caught me a little off guard, and I didn't answer immediately.

"Sorry, Jack. I didn't mean to be so personal."

"No, please, don't be sorry. Just surprised me, that's all. Caught me off guard." My answer came from the heart. "Sure. I enjoy the work."

"I just noticed your mood changes from time to time. You know, as if work has somehow gotten you down or something."

"Maybe at times, it can feel a little stale." I

pondered the question again and wondered just how close to the mark she really was. "But for the most part, it's what I know. I don't think I could do much else. Everyone's different, but I couldn't do an office job. Sitting in an office, writing notes, and taking calls would be a nightmare for me. And could you imagine me in a customer service role? Those poor customers wouldn't know what hit them." I shivered at the thought of sitting through meeting after meeting, listening to someone drone on about something I had no interest in. "I wouldn't last a week in customer service."

"Don't flatter yourself—you wouldn't last a day," she joked. "Do you like helping guys like Mark Costa? Or does that really get under your skin?"

"He gets under my skin," I said. It was uncanny how close to the truth she was. "Guys like Mark just don't do it for me. The thought of helping someone like that with whatever they have going on isn't what I had ever planned for."

"And yet here you are."

She was right. Of course, she was. It wasn't the first time either, although this time, she was right about something that had become a lot more than my livelihood. My work had become my life, more so since I lost Claire. It was a revelation I hadn't expected to be pointed out so bluntly to me. Casey must have seen my expression change.

"I'm sorry if that's a little too personal. I didn't mean to pry."

I smiled and tried to show her it wasn't bothering me. "Perhaps you're right. Maybe my life has taken a slow turn towards darker pastures."

"Isn't there anything else you've ever wanted to

do, though? Any other career?"

I tried to think, but knew the answer almost immediately. It was the same answer I'd been telling myself my entire adult life.

"Unless I could play the guitar all day, then there aren't many other things I'd love to do," I said. "I don't do well working for someone else and that rules out a lot of options. And besides, I love being an investigator. It's in my blood. And I have a pretty good partner." I smiled and then, as if trying to back up my argument, I added, "And it has more than paid the bills up until now."

She took a couple of steps ahead of me, spun and faced me as she walked backward. With her arms held out to amplify her words, she said, "Haven't you ever dreamed of something more? Come on, there must be something that you've wanted to do."

"Haven't you?"

"We're not talking about me here, Jack."

"No, but I've seen you as well, you know? I can see the fire in your eyes some days reduced down to bare cinders."

"Yeah, sure." She reneged a little. "I've got dreams, and one day, I'll fulfill them. But you're ahead of me by a few years and you don't appear to be wanting anything else."

"It's taken me time to deal with things."

That was when I saw her own grief come forward again. Not a lot, but enough to tell me that the subject was a little too close to home. Casey turned back and fell in beside me, watching as we passed a young mother and her toddlers. The older child was a boy, while the younger girl chased her brother around and around, the whole time giggling at the top of her lungs. The mother looked at us, a little embarrassed. Casey shot her a smile as we walked by.

"You miss Rhys, don't you?" I said, shifting away from the career advice for the time being.

"Every day." She didn't hesitate in her answer. "Some days are definitely worse than others. Much worse."

"I know. When I was going through the worst of it after the shooting, Troy was the one that would drop by, hang out and just listen when I needed to talk. It took a long time for me to be able to go a day without feeling it. I don't think I still really do."

"Guess I've had a bit more time to deal with things than you, but yes, I doubt we'll ever truly learn to deal with it completely. Not deep down, anyway. But maybe that's just how it's supposed to be." She shrugged. "The fact that Rhys died alone in a park after falling over has haunted me many nights. That thought cuts me deep inside."

We continued on in silence for a little further.

"What I've learned about loss is that it makes us appreciate the here and now much more." Casey folded her arms across her chest. "There's no guarantee of a tomorrow, not for any of us."

I agreed and perhaps understood why she began questioning my future career options in the first place. It was her nurturing instincts trying to protect me.

"There's nothing more I love than the rush of danger in this job," I added as we reached the edge of the park. "And I'm sure if we keep digging, then this case will fulfill my every wish."

CHAPTER 19

WITH ALL the probing and investigating that had been going on, I shouldn't have been shocked by what happened next. It surprised me that it didn't happen sooner. It came during the mid-afternoon, five minutes past three, with Casey and I sitting around my desk, discussing the theories we'd been working on. We were working on a way to sneak into Mindy's apartment to check for the laptop.

The inner door to my office had remained open during our meeting. We had no appointments scheduled, and with just the two of us there, it seemed pointless to close it. Plus, walk-ins weren't something that happened too often, not with the rise of the internet and cellphone technology.

But suddenly, the outer door to our office was slammed shut loudly enough for Casey to jump in her seat. Then I heard my name screamed as it rose through the building, and Mark Costa charged through the doorway.

"Jack Valentine!" He was fuming, that much was obvious. Guys like that struggled to contain their emotions. "Where are you?"

I remained seated, leaned back, and waited for him to find us. It wasn't too difficult considering the foyer only led to a single office and a kitchenette. He walked through the doorway a split second later, and when he saw me sitting at my desk, he launched into his tirade.

"What have you done?! How does my father know the laptop has gone missing?" His arms began waving about, as if he was also trying to mime his way through the conversation. He pointed his finger at me. "This is your fault. This is all your fault. You shouldn't have talked to him."

His words floated over my head, none of them coming close to riling me up. His temper wasn't about to get a rise out of me either, and I simply sat and waited for him to finish. Unfortunately for Casey, that meant she had to remain seated until he finished as well because I wasn't about to interrupt him. That would've caused a defensive response, and I needed him to get everything out of his system.

"Well?" he continued. "Are you going to answer me? Or are you just going to sit there and hope the laptop falls out of the sky?"

Only once I knew his rage had run out of steam did I talk, but not to him, something that surprised the man.

"Would you give us a moment?" I said to Casey, and she nodded before heading out to the reception area and closing the door, leaving us alone for the time being. Once she was gone, I turned my attention back to Mark Costa.

"You should sit down," I said just as calmly. For a brief moment, I didn't think he was going to sit. His nostrils were flaring, like a bull still fired up from his previous charge. He paced back and forth, his eyes fixed on mine. But when he realized that I wasn't going to be drawn into a screaming match, he did sit on the edge of the chair, waiting for me to respond.

Once I knew he was calm enough to listen, I began to speak.

"I'm not in the habit of revealing critical information to suspects." It looked as if he was about to launch into a second tirade, but when I held a hand up, he swallowed hard and snapped his mouth shut. I leaned forward for a bit of effect. "It wouldn't take your father long to figure it out, however. Especially if his son hired a private investigator. And what if the item stolen from his apartment was one of the most valuable things he owned and thus a great big clue for anybody watching?"

He didn't like my answer and went to stand up again. I waved him down, and after considering, he complied.

"You think this is my fault?" he snapped. "You think I brought this on myself?"

I didn't need to answer, but I did anyway. "The moment you hired me was the moment you made it clear that the burglary had netted the culprit something far more valuable than dispensable items." I thought this point was quite obvious, but it turned out, Mark Costa wasn't up to speed on the subject. "It was only a matter of time before your father figured it out."

"If you hadn't talked to my father, he may have never known about it. This is your fault. What did you say to him?"

"It doesn't matter what we talked about. He has ears on the ground. He's still a man with a lot of connections, and it wouldn't take him long to piece the puzzle together."

Mark Costa took a breath and leaned back in his chair. For a moment, I thought he was going to start again, perhaps down a new path to vent his frustrations, but he didn't. He leaned forward, resting his head in his hands, shaking at the thought of losing his business.

"He was all up in my face this morning, yelling and screaming and carrying on. He almost broke the door to my office when he charged through it. He threatened me and told me not to contact him. He said he was back in the game now, and I was just a little boy with a weak arm. He then went on a rant about how disappointed he was in me—all the way from my baseball days to my business days. He really dug in."

"He said he was back in the game?"

"That's what he said. He has plans to get back into property development. He wants to destroy me." He stood and rubbed his hand along his brow. "He said that he was no longer going to let me control his life and that it was high time he returned to the industry he knew best. He wants the money, and he wants the power. He always loved to be in control. He said that without my advantage, he would run right over me."

"'Without your advantage.' I think we both know what that means."

"You think that he means the laptop?"

"What did you think it meant?"

"I think—" He hesitated and looked a little confused as he ran the conversation through his mind. "I thought he meant that I already had a company up and running, and if he started a new company, he would beat mine."

"Could be. But from where I'm sitting, it sounds as if he's talking about the laptop. It's the advantage you hold over him. And as for the company, something tells me he isn't about to start a new one."

"He's still got a lot of connections in the development industry. Some of my guys are still loyal to him, and there's a lot of people that want me gone." He looked at me as if it was the first time he entertained the idea of losing the company. "You think he's powerful enough to take the firm from me? You think he would try and do that?"

I nodded, but I couldn't believe he was asking the question.

"You need to watch yourself, Valentine," he continued after dismissing the thought. "My father is dangerous. He won't hesitate to come looking for you if he thinks you're a threat to him."

"I know what a man like your father is capable of. Not my first rodeo."

He paced the floor for a few moments before I decided to ask a question of my own, expecting an honest answer because of his mood at that point. It felt as if he'd dropped his guard.

"Mark, how well do you really know Mindy Fox?"

"Mindy?" He raised his eyebrows. "It wasn't her. I've told you this already. She had nothing to do with it. I can't believe you're wasting your time still chasing her. I told you that it wasn't her. How many times do I have to explain that to you?"

"Her name keeps coming up, and that's the way this investigation is heading. We were just sitting here talking about how to get into her apartment and search the place. We know this was an inside job, and it's starting to look more and more like she has all the access needed. Right now, she's suspect number one."

"No, not Mindy. Look, I'm not stupid when it comes to her." He ran his hand across his brow. "Ok.

I'm coming clean to you. I'll tell you the truth—I know everything about her. I did my research before I started spending time with her. I know she takes the things I give her and pawns them. I know she needs money. I didn't know if the story about her mother was real, but I didn't care about that. Hell, I even know she has a boyfriend. It's that stupid Russian security guard downstairs. The guy's an idiot, but he's harmless."

That surprised me. I didn't expect him to know that information. "I'm not sure that he's harmless."

"Maybe." He paced the floor again before he stopped and looked at me. "Jack, you need to do what needs to be done. It's what I'm paying you for. I need you to stop at nothing to get that laptop back."

"Do you think your father is involved?"

"I'm telling you, right now, this has my father's fingerprints all over it. He's behind this, and that's where your attention should be focused." He walked to the door and tapped his head against it. When he opened the door, he looked back to me and added, "I need that laptop back. Whatever it takes. And I need it now."

He didn't bother waiting for a reply. He turned and walked back out into the reception area. He paused beside Casey, said something I couldn't hear, then continued out through the door. Moments later, Casey rejoined me in the office.

"That was tense," she said as she sat. "What did you say to him?"

"Nothing major, but that was also quite informative. Sergio knows about the missing laptop, and I don't think he's going to be as welcoming the next time I go to see him."

I repeated everything that Mark Costa and I had discussed, and Casey listened with the same interest as she always did. Once I was finished, we continued to bounce ideas around, just as we'd been doing before Mark's sudden interruption. The only difference was, now we had a little extra insight into other possibilities.

I couldn't let go of the Triad connection. There had to be more to it than what I had uncovered, and although I didn't mention it to Mark, I needed to follow up on that line of questioning. I decided that the best course of action was to go and speak to someone I knew would have some inside information about the notorious Chinese outfit. Former undercover detective, and now a fellow investigator, Sam Wong had decades of investigative experience with criminal gangs and was the perfect person to give me the inside scoop.

Once Casey and I had finished our latest exchange, she headed out to track Mindy's movements, leaving me free to pursue my own line of investigation. I shot Wong a message and asked him if he was up for a catch-up, then jumped on the internet while I waited for his response.

He answered a little after five, with just two simple words: 'Yes. Frankie's.'

The hotdog stand was a favorite of mine. It served a foot-long sausage, crafted together with a mixture of relish, sauerkraut, mustard, and love. I sent a thumbs-up emoji back, then closed up shop before heading downstairs.

CHAPTER 20

THE DRIVE to the lakeside hotdog vendor took a little longer thanks to a traffic accident on the I90, but after taking a quick detour through a number of neighborhood streets, I managed to get back on track a little further along. By the time I reached the parking lot in Jackson Park, I had spotted Sam Wong's familiar Dodge.

"Still got Bess, I see?" I called out when I saw Sam Wong.

Bess was Wong's 1977 Dodge Challenger, his pride and joy, complete with all the chrome trimmings and vinyl roof. Standing near it in black slacks, polished shoes, and a white shirt, Sam Wong looked like he could still be a detective. When working in the PD, he was an easy choice to send undercover for any Chinese connection—his parents were Chinese, he'd traveled there as a child, and he was fluent in Mandarin. He looked younger than his years, his soft skin not displaying the amount of pain and agony he'd seen in his twenty-five years as a detective in Chicago. He left the force soon after he came out of an undercover sting gone wrong, and moved into becoming a private investigator. He fed me information in the past while in the force, and I'd done the same for him. Despite being a potential career rival, I was happy to help him adjust and move into the world of private investigations. I didn't see him as a work competitor because he worked exclusively with insurance firms. And that was the sort of work I avoided at all costs.

"I'll have her forever," he said, shaking hands with me and pointing towards the familiar eatery. "It's good to see you, Jack. You working hard, or hardly working?"

"I'm working hard. Always," I said, seeing the extra tables and chairs the owner had set up. "This place has really expanded."

"Not run by Frankie anymore," Wong said, shocking me with the news.

"What? No." Frankie Delaney had been iconic in this part of the world, a true gentleman who made his devoted customers laugh over many years. "Retired?" I asked, hopeful for a positive answer. Wong's expression told me otherwise.

"Died in his sleep."

"Man," I said, saddened by the news. "When?"

"Couple of years ago. His daughter runs it now. Said he was planning to retire to Florida the following summer, but it never came to be. Worked himself to death."

"That really blows. Stella?"

Wong nodded. Stella was one of Frankie's five daughters. He was a classic Italian father, and his legendary status went much deeper than just the local neighborhood. As we waited in line behind a Chinese family for our order, we could see that it wasn't Stella that was serving either. The stranger was a young girl of maybe fifteen, looking sheepish as she tried to take the order from the family.

"How's work?" I asked, making conversation to

pass the time.

"Not bad. Lots of insurance claims made by idiots. So many people are out there trying to make a quick buck off their insurance policy, but what they're doing is criminal. They're setting the companies up to try and make a quick dollar. They don't want to work for the money; they just want an easy way to retire. A lot of the claims are clearly fraudulent. I don't have sympathy for the insurance companies, most of them are worth hundreds of millions of dollars, but I'll never approve of fraud by anyone."

"You ever think you'll go back to the PD?"

"No chance," Wong shook his head, then looked up to see the family finally done and heading for one of the tables. "After I went undercover, I could never work for the PD again. Too much corruption inside those walls."

The girl took our order, although at first, she struggled to understand what we meant when we said, 'Frankie's Dogs.' For anyone who had spent any amount of time in the place, they would've known instantly. But the girl was just as new as the cook standing behind her, and thus neither knew of the hotdog that had made Frankie's famous in these parts.

We waited for our order, then grabbed a seat by the water. While the dogs were far from what I remembered, they still weren't bad, and I could've easily ordered a second. But I pushed the temptation aside and simply sipped my Coke as Wong finished the rest of his.

"You always did stuff your food down your throat as if being chased by a pack of hungry wolves," Wong laughed. "You should slow down a little."

"Just happen to enjoy my food a little more than most," I smiled. "It gives me more time to focus on work."

"I'm guessing that's why I'm here. You didn't call me down here just for a foot-long and a Coke, did you?"

Straight to the point. It's what I liked about the man.

"You're right. I wanted to pick your brain a little more about Lee Chan."

He nodded almost immediately. "Somehow, I knew you wouldn't let that one lie still. I had a feeling Lee Chan was going to be in your life one way or another one day."

He didn't know just how right he was.

The Chinese family was eating their food near the main ordering window, and an unpleasant exchange had begun between the cook and the father. He was sending a tirade of abuse towards where the cook was leaning out of the window. For a moment, I thought he was going to jump right out of the window and launch himself at the screaming man, but the family finally began to move off, the wife trying to drag her husband away from the scene. We simply sat and watched as they made their departure.

"Hair in the hotdog," the father said as he stormed away. "Who allows that to happen?"

I shook my head. This was a place where good food came cheap and fast, and errors were to be expected, but I guess some people's expectations were higher than others.

"Who are you working for?" Wong asked.

"Mark Costa."

Wong pursed his lips and whistled. "Are you sure

you want to do that, Jack? That's poking the beast and stepping into a dangerous world. The Costa's are not a nice family."

"I'm working a burglary that wasn't solved by the cops," I said. "It's my job to follow the evidence trail. It's leading me to the Lee Chan connection."

"Be careful," Wong added. "Whatever was stolen must be important if Mark Costa has you hunting around for it."

I nodded.

"And you want to know if I know something about it?"

"Sam, you were always the guy with the most information around here. This was your world for so long, and I'm sure you still know a thing or two about these guys."

"I've kept my finger on the pulse, and I heard something this morning that might be of interest to you," Wong continued, and my ears pricked up. "I was talking to a contact, and he was giving me an update about the gangs that operate in Chinatown. Word is that Lee Chan was working with Mark Costa, but it appears he has another business partner, someone who approached him with a new proposal."

To be honest, I half expected him to tell me that Mindy Fox had somehow tracked the Triads down, considered selling some secrets from her financially well-off pseudo-boyfriend, and maybe make a few bucks from the deal. But that wasn't how Wong's information played out.

"Who is it?"

"Sergio Costa."

"Are you sure he's involved with Lee Chan?"

"Rumor is that Sergio Costa isn't completely

finished with his property-development ideas. The corrupt old man wants to take the firm back from his son."

I was shocked but not entirely surprised by the news. The man had already announced his intended return, and honing in on Mark's partners would have been the next logical move.

Mark Costa had been right about more things than he realized. His father was trying to retake his property development business. He was also extremely unpredictable, and now, with Lee Chan and the Triads in his corner, he'd also become unbelievably dangerous, not just to me, but to everyone else as well.

"Sergio is ruthless," I said. "Do you think he has it in him to murder his own son?"

"No, they're family. They don't do that." Wong looked out across the water as he considered the question. I actually thought he would scoff at the idea, saying that the father would never go that far. But watching him actually consider the question frightened me. Maybe he knew more than he was letting on. "I've known Sergio Costa for a long time, and part of that has been because of his dealings with criminal organizations. He's volatile, unpredictable, and not afraid to make hard decisions. There are also rumors that the man has been involved in no less than half a dozen disappearances, but his own son? No, I don't think he would kill him. He'd lock his son in a cage for the rest of his life, but he wouldn't pull the trigger."

I considered telling Wong everything at that moment, about the laptop and everything else I discovered, but part of me knew I couldn't. There was too much at stake, and throwing further rumors into the mix wasn't going to help anybody. If anything, it would just confuse things even more.

"Do you think he'll kill others to take over the business again?" Part of me wanted to believe that nothing like that could ever really happen, but part of me knew that Sergio Costa was the sort of man that would deal with murder in the same cold-hearted manner he conducted everything else.

"He's a killer, no doubt about it. All of the people he's rumored to have murdered, or ordered the hit on, had a history with him in one way or another. Whether it was directly related to his construction business or personal matters, the guy just has a habit of showing up in police investigations. And now with Lee Chan behind him? That storm is only just beginning, and it's going to be thunderous."

"How deep does Sergio's involvement go with Chan right now? Is it already at a handshake stage, or is it just being planned out?"

"From what I've heard, it appears that Sergio Costa plans on taking over from where his son failed. My guess is that once Sergio has control over that side of the business, he'll throw Mark to the buzzards and not care what they leave behind. He'll throw his son out on the street, but he just won't kill him." He rolled his tongue around his mouth for a moment. "But I think if Sergio goes to work for Lee Chan, then I doubt Chan would go after Mark Costa. Swapping out one Costa for another is probably a good deal for Chan. So in terms of his business, Mark Costa is a dead man walking, simply biding his time until the reaper comes knocking."

"Mark Costa is not going to go down without a

fight," I said. "He thinks it's his business, and he won't hand it back over to his father, no matter how nicely he asks. He'll fight to the very end."

"Then the clock is ticking," Wong said. "Sergio was always a fast mover. If there was a chance, he'd take it. I imagine that he's using some of the Triad's muscle right now to gain some of his old contracts back. It's only a matter of time before things turn volatile."

I'd heard enough, and for me, it gave even more indication that Sergio was the man who had taken the laptop.

While Mindy may have had a monetary motivation to steal it, Sergio had much more to gain by getting ahold of that laptop. He had his very livelihood on the line, and there was more than just pride at stake. For Sergio, that video footage held the power to either return his business empire to him, or swallow him up completely.

"Thank you, my friend," I said, rising to my feet. "It's always good to see you."

"Any time, Jack. And if I can give you a word of advice?"

"Of course." I nodded as we shook hands.

Wong's advice was something I accepted without question. He'd proven himself countless times, and I trusted him.

"Watch yourself around Sergio Costa and the Triads. If he has any indication that you're coming after him for something, regardless of how minor, there'll be some serious consequences." He grimaced a little at the thought of the consequences. "You're in a dangerous world, and you're playing with a very hot fire, Jack. Watch where you step."

CHAPTER 21

CASEY SHOWED up to the office at five minutes before eight the next morning, where I was waiting with two coffees. After a brief recap of the previous day's events and meetings, I threw out the idea that there was perhaps one way of finding out what Sergio Costa was really up to.

"The storage unit," I said. "We have to know what's inside there. If he's taken possession of the laptop, he may be keeping it in there."

"Wouldn't he just destroy it?" Casey floated the idea. "If he took possession of it, he'd destroy it in a heartbeat. It'd be gone, and so would all his problems."

"Then why did he rent the storage unit near Mark's apartment? The timing fits," I said, and then a thought crossed my mind. "We know that Mark Costa hasn't been truthful with us for most of this case. We know he's been lying to us, and not giving us all the information. Maybe, just maybe, the video footage also implicates Mark in the murder."

"That makes sense," Casey nodded. "Because it'd be a way for Sergio to blackmail his son out of the business. Maybe it's Mark that actually pulled the trigger in the murder of the man in the alley and Sergio was the accessory, and Mark threatened to take them both down unless Sergio handed over the keys to the business."

"It's a good theory. Mark is the type of man who would risk everything to get an advantage," I said. "It's time we had a look inside that storage unit to see just what his father is up to for real. If he hired Mindy to steal it, then that could be where he's keeping it. Now that he's got nothing to lose, he might be returning the favor to his son."

"What a mess," Casey replied, not one to shy away from the manual labor of the job. "When do you want to go?"

"Now," I suggested, and she nodded.

We decided to go in Casey's Mini this time, so I could confirm the details on my cell, as well as find out where Sergio Costa was at that very moment. The last thing we needed was for the man to show up right as we were breaking into his storage unit. Break-ins went a whole lot better when the owner wasn't around.

A quick phone call to his restaurant was all it took for me to confirm his whereabouts. I called, pretending to be a magazine reporter for one of the country's most prestigious foodie publications. I remembered his reaction the last time he thought I was a reporter. The woman that answered the call said the owner would be interested in an interview and gave me his home phone number. I called Sergio's home phone and a young woman answered. I didn't ask who she was, and I didn't want to know. There seemed to be something about the Costa men and young women. I explained the spiel about being a reporter to her, and she said she'd get Sergio on the phone right away. I didn't doubt her for a second. When she called for Sergio and he yelled something back, I had my answer, and the phone line went dead.

The self-storage center turned out to be quite lax in the way of security, and it made our job so much simpler. For a start, the entrance boom gate was already up, as a flatbed had parked immediately behind it and appeared to be loading up several pallets of what could've been abandoned items. We drove straight in and parked at the farthest corner of the lot.

Because the flatbed owners were ferrying goods out by the truckload from several lockers, the front doors were also wide open, held in place by a couple of bricks. There was an employee standing nearby, but he was in a deep conversation with the driver of the truck, both looking very displeased with each other. We used the altercation to our advantage.

"55E," Casey whispered to me as we cleared the final hurdle, with nothing but open corridors between us and our destination. Each aisle had a numbered allocation, and where we'd entered the building, the number five had been painted repeatedly along the floor.

This wasn't where the wealthy stored anything of value—this was where people who could only afford a locker stored their excess junk. If there was anything valuable kept here, I imagine that it'd disappear within the first five hours.

We continued walking, with some of the garage-sized lockers standing open and people rummaging through. I was worried that we might not have the privacy we needed to gain entry, given the amount of foot traffic we'd already seen.

But we needn't have worried. Aisle 55 stood in one of the furthest locations and held some of the largest lockers available. As it was, we were the only ones to walk along that part of the building. There were no cameras on the ceiling, and part of me wondered just how secure these places really were. I set myself a mental reminder to never trust a place like this with anything I considered as worth keeping.

We passed Aisle 55 Locker A and quickly continued along the corridor. Each locker door was the size of a small car garage, and I could only imagine the kinds of things being stored in each one. Once we reached the one marked with a large E, I knew my lock picking skills were due for a workout.

There were two simple slide bolts in the bottom corners of the door, with a single padlock on each. I took out my picking kit, selected the tool I needed, and went to work. Casey kept a look out.

It'd been a while since I'd used these skills, but just like riding a bike, they never seemed to fade. I did have a good teacher; God rest her soul, a woman named Marilyn Capone. She was a fiery Italian, with lungs the size of Wisconsin. Her laughter could be heard several blocks away and when she spoke, you made a habit of listening. She liked to tell those who didn't know better that she was related to Al Capone and marveled at how people treated her, as if she was criminal royalty. But she told me the truth one time— she had no known connections to the infamous mobster.

Marilyn Capone had been what you might call a good old-fashioned lock-picker. She'd done jobs with several outfits, although I'm not sure you could call them gangs. They used her unique services whenever they wanted to knock off a house, a bank, or a private company. Marilyn would show up first, do her work, and leave while the rest of them filled their bags.

She'd gotten caught only once by yours truly when I was hired by a hardware store in Peoria, Central Illinois to find the crew that broke into the store. The man who had hired me for that job had been referred by a friend who had used my services the previous summer. Marilyn ended up serving time and I felt sorry for her, so I had made it a habit to drop by on occasion to visit her here and there. She was so grateful that by the time she was released a few years later, she kept in touch, and each time we caught up, she would continue teaching me about the fine art of lock picking. She was pushing almost sixty by then, a true veteran of her craft. What she taught me became invaluable in my line of work, and when she passed a few years ago, she'd left me one final package to remember her by.

The small package had contained a set of picks that she'd been using for going on forty-five years. Her father had gifted her the set, himself an illusionist whose primary form of entertainment was escaping.

As I sat with the set of tools laid out before me, carefully picking the lock on the metal padlocks, Marilyn's voice kept playing through my mind, booming in all its ferocity, just the way it had during her living years.

"Remember, Jackie," she said, calling me the name she had chosen the first time we met. "Finesse, patience, and a small slice of positivity is all you need." The last one was key, she had said often, because a lot of pickers would lose their cool, not realizing that they may have been just moments away from filling their pockets.

Each lock fell open in my hands barely a few

seconds after I went to work, and before you could say open sesame, we were standing inside the darkened locker.

Casey pulled out her phone and lit up the screen enough for us to get a little light. I ran my hands along the edges of the unit, and after a few moments of fumbling around, I felt the light switch.

The contents of the locker surprised me as the fluorescent light flickered into life. There was nothing but a single cardboard box sitting in the middle of the floor, perhaps large enough to hold a set of dishes. Casey and I looked at each other as we took a step towards it, unsure of what would be waiting inside it.

"Think it's booby-trapped?" She asked just as I neared it, and to be honest, the comment gave me a reason to pause. Given what we knew about Sergio Costa, the prospect wasn't entirely out of the question. Perhaps he knew we would come looking for the laptop, and he left this here especially for us, thinking we'd be dumb enough to take a look. As it turned out, he would've been right.

"Stay back," I whispered, unsure of whether my mind was playing tricks or whether it was foretelling our immediate future. After telling myself that it was just my mind playing tricks, I took a deep breath then knelt down to lift open one flap.

The box's contents turned out to be an even bigger anticlimax than finding a nearly empty locker.

"It's pasta sauce," I said, lifting one tin out for Casey to see.

"Pasta sauce?" she took a step forward to confirm. She peered inside and let out a sigh. My thoughts exactly.

"There's nothing here," I conceded. With the

locker standing empty before us and a box that proved just as useless, I knew that this had been pretty much a bust. "Let's get out of here."

There was little else we could do and staying any longer than we needed to just put us at more risk of getting caught. We killed the lights before I slid the door up again, made sure there was nobody watching, then quickly returned the padlocks to their previous location once the door was slid closed again.

"At least we know it's empty," Casey said as we walked back out of the building. "But it had to be a set-up."

"That's right," I looked over my shoulder. "Did you see anyone watching us as we came in?"

"No one," she shook her head. "But I wasn't looking that hard."

"It's either a decoy to throw us off the trail, or they're watching us. If the locker had a silent alarm, they could've been notified that we'd opened it," I kept Casey at my side, unconsciously shielding her from any open space. "And that means we should get out of here."

The uniformed employee was still talking to the truck driver as we passed, and when he shot me a wave, I returned it with a smile. Nobody paid us the slightest attention and once we were back at the car, we climbed in and drove out the front gate.

I kept checking over my shoulder as Casey drove down the road, watching each passing car with intensity. None made a swerve at us. It appeared we were in the clear.

"Time for something to eat?" Casey asked. "We're far enough away from the place."

I nodded.

There was a Vietnamese vendor set up in a small parking lot outside an abandoned shop, and Casey pointed out that we needed something a little healthier than meatball subs. For once, I agreed with her.

As Casey parked her Mini, I couldn't shake the troubled feeling that had been building. Everything about this case felt uneasy and I pictured myself walking around with a blindfold on. Most cases didn't have this many dead ends, and yet this one proved to have nothing but. It began to feel like someone was playing us.

Casey parked across the street from the vendor.

We were waiting to cross the quiet road when I saw something hurtling towards us. There were motorbikes. Two of them.

I grabbed Casey's arm just as she was about to cross the street, holding her back to wait. We stood by her Mini as the bikes hurtled towards us.

They weren't slowing.

"Move!" I pushed Casey behind the Mini, off the road, before jumping out of the way.

The two-wheeled riders roared close to us.

Too close to be safe. Too close for an accident.

Once they were past us, I stared as they raced down the road.

The bikes neither stopped, nor reacted, to what had just happened, and I was sure that one of the riders I saw was Asian. The helmet's visor had been pulled up and the eyes were clearly visible through the gap.

"Was that intentional?" Casey asked. "Do you think they knew us?"

"I think so," I said. Whatever hunger I had felt

was gone, and I knew that the better option was to get out of there.

"Do you think they'll come back?" Casey looked at me. I looked up the road to where the bikes had gone but couldn't see any sign of them.

"We should get back in the car and keep moving." I wasn't taking any chances and jumped back into the car. She insisted on driving, and I agreed.

Casey didn't need to be asked twice to hurry up and moments later, we were back in traffic, although this time, I directed Casey to a less obvious route to get back to the office.

Her hands were shaking more than I was comfortable with and after suggesting that it might be better for me to drive, she didn't argue, pulling over just long enough for us to swap sides.

As I strapped myself into the driver's seat, I regretted not taking the truck. At least if we were in that, we would have substantially more weight behind us, just in case the bikes returned for a little more action.

Casey checked her handgun was loaded, then looked at me and nodded.

It was time to go.

CHAPTER 22

RATHER THAN head west, I decided the better option would be to go the opposite way, and so I turned east instead. My plan was to head all the way into the central district, then hop onto the Interstate and go back the long way.

I'd also decided that it might be better to head back to the office than go home. At least there, we'd be surrounded by more people, and the cameras of the building itself would keep a watchful eye. At our homes, we'd be more vulnerable. The traffic was heavy as we made our way towards the lakeside district. Casey looked nervously at the traffic surrounding us, turning around constantly to peer out through the back window. I could hear her holding her breath whenever a motorbike neared us, but each time, it turned out to be nothing more than a fellow road user.

"Why are we risking our lives for the laptop?" Casey whispered, more to herself than me.

"Because this is the world we work in," I said. "This is the underworld; this is the criminal world that not many people get to experience. If we want to get paid, these are the people we have to deal with."

"It's not all about money."

"You're right. Honor and integrity come first. That's why we have to do our job and find that laptop," I paused before I continued, "And then we have to find a way to convict Sergio Costa and Mark Costa of murder."

Casey didn't respond. She stared out the window, watching the world go past. I wasn't sure that she was convinced by my statement.

"How did they find us?" Casey questioned. "We weren't close to the location, and we weren't using your truck."

"Maybe they got lucky and spotted us as we took the turn off the Interstate," I responded, checking out the rearview mirror again. "Bikes move a lot quicker than cars; they could've been zipping through the traffic once they knew the unit had been opened."

Twenty-five minutes into our journey, our nerves began to subside again, with Casey relaxing enough to thumb the radio to life. She played with the dial for a bit before settling on some classic rock, the Eagles singing about that famous hotel.

I was drumming my fingers on the steering wheel as I spotted the Interstate's onramp, and once I turned the small car onto it, I breathed easier. This was perhaps not as bad as I had imagined. Perhaps given our circumstances, we'd blown the incident up into way more than it deserved. Not entirely out of the question.

The traffic was a lot more congested than I'd hoped for, but with no sign of the motorcycles, I figured it would be a chance for us to gather our thoughts.

"Maybe we got it wrong," Casey said. "Maybe that was just a coincidence. Maybe they weren't trying to hit us."

It may have been an unrelated incident, and given

our situation, it was perhaps an easy mistake to make. Traffic incidents weren't exactly a rare occurrence in the city.

But just as I was about to agree with Casey, I spotted familiar movement coming up behind us, and as I took a closer look in the rearview mirror, my insides tightened. There were two bikes, moving between the cars like they were hunting prey on the Interstate.

"Hang on," I whispered, "It looks like we've got company."

Casey turned in her seat to take a look and then pulled the loaded gun out of her handbag. Her eyes were focused. She'd gone into action-mode.

"One's got a gun," she called out. "Coming on your left."

I had just enough time to spot the weapon in my side mirror before the motorbike pulled up inches from my window.

I swerved in that direction, hit the gas pedal, and called for Casey to get down. I'd lost sight of the second bike, with the rider moving to the other side of the car. There was a Ford pickup on that side, and I knew I could use that to my advantage.

The Mini had more power than I had expected, and when I punched the engine, it kicked up a gear, pulling slightly ahead of the bikes. It gave us enough time to spot the two pursuers before they tried to hide again in the adjoining traffic.

"Who are they?" Casey called, now turned in her seat and facing backward. She was ready to fire.

"I think they're Lee Chan's crew," I said, my eyes darting everywhere, analyzing the traffic ahead.

There were a couple of SUVs directly ahead, as

well as in the lane to my left. In the right lane, the same lane where one of the motorbikes was moving, was a semi-truck around two to three hundred yards further up. As we continued to accelerate, the distance was closing fast.

There was a gap between the SUV and the truck, and the closer we got, the smaller the gap became. The SUV was traveling just a little faster, as well as driving more to the right side of their lane. It didn't leave a lot of space between them, but I knew I had to take the risk.

Planting the gas pedal even harder, I aimed for the gap as it continued to close.

The bike was off my rear fender. If I managed to squeeze through, the rider would need to slow enough to either pass the SUV on the left, or slow down even further to make his way around to the other side of the truck, perhaps taking the breakdown lane.

As I made a dash for the shrinking gap between the SUV and truck, one thought ran through my mind. If I misjudged it, we would end up underneath the massive rig and perhaps run over by the trailer. The Mini was no match for the semi. But just as I was preparing to make the final move, the rider to the left had made his way closer to the back of our car.

He'd been riding in the shadows of a pickup, and when we were distracted by his partner, he'd crept out and made a beeline for my blind spot.

The sound of the gunshot was loud, and the explosion of rear window glass left little doubt as to their true intent.

The rider fired a second time, and the bullet hit the back door. The third bullet blew out the rear seat window on Casey's side, sending glass shards onto the road.

Casey aimed to fire back, but a missed shot could go anywhere and hit anyone on the Interstate. Despite the incoming bullets, she remained calm and focused.

It could've easily gone either way, but when the rider fired a fourth time, he threw the balance in our favor by accident. I heard the pop of the pistol, then I heard the bullet come flying through the cabin of the car. It exited the vehicle, continued on, and hit one of the truck's trailer tires.

The explosion of rubber peppered the Mini's hood and windshield, loud enough that for a split second, I thought the tire debris would cave it in. But when I saw the black shrapnel bounce harmlessly off, I knew we were saved. I couldn't say the same for the other two.

When truck tires shred, they leave a debris field a mile long.

The huge strips of rubber bounced behind the truck, scattering in a thousand directions. The rider had no time to react before hitting the largest of the pieces caused havoc.

It became airborne for a brief flash, tangled in the front tire of the bike and flipped it slightly sideways. As it touched back down, the trajectory of the bike had shifted enough for the rider to lose all sense of control. The bike hit the road hard, rolled over and bucked the rider clean off, sending him sliding down the asphalt as the bike showered sparks in all directions.

The second rider slowed and pulled up next to the fallen rider, who remained motionless on the road. Other vehicles began to stop, and before long, we'd lost sight of them as we continued on, never slowing until we eventually pulled off a few exits later.

We were lucky this time, but I wasn't sure how long that luck would last.

CHAPTER 23

AS WE drove away, my guess was that enough drivers had seen what happened, and they would've called the cops. If the downed rider was injured, it would at least give us enough time to make our escape. Rather than pull over, I continued on until we were well outside the normal range of our office. If anybody had still been following us, I doubt they would've remained on our tail.

We made our way to Casey's apartment in Logan Square, checking over our shoulders the whole time. The back window of the car had been blown out, but Casey lived two doors down from a repair shop, and once she turned on her natural charm with the older mechanics, they said they'd have it fixed in a few hours. They didn't ask about the bullet hole in the side-view mirror and Casey didn't tell them.

We decided against going to the cops. It would've been no use and would've only further restricted our movements concerning the case. We were so close to the truth—that much was obvious—and if we wanted to close the case, then we had to keep going. The questions from the authorities would've only complicated the matter.

Casey was mostly calm. She was a little shaken up, but she did her best to hide it. After we dropped the car at the repair shop, we walked back to her apartment as the sun started to climb to its highest point of the day. We settled in, and Casey poured two whiskeys. We sat on the rear balcony, looking over the park nearby.

"It might be only 11:55am, but I think we deserve this drink," Casey said as she sipped her whiskey. "We've earned it today."

"And hopefully, that's the last we've seen of them. I don't think they'll miss next time."

"But why would they come after us like that? Haven't they already made their point? What was the purpose of trying to chase us off the road now?"

"I'm not sure, but if I had to guess, I'd say Lee Chan thinks I know more than I actually do." I was embarrassed. "Maybe it wasn't such a good idea to pay him a visit."

"You think? You're a smart guy, Jack. Real with it," she mocked, and I deserved it. "This is supposed to be nothing more than a hunt for a stolen laptop, not an international spy operation against the Chinese Mafia. You stepped into the wrong criminal gang."

"I know, I know." My cheeks burned as she scolded me. "I'm sorry. If I had my time over, I would've played it differently with Lee Chan."

"What do we do now?"

"For the moment, we sit tight. I'll contact—"

My cell vibrated in my pocket. It was a text from an unknown number, but the message was loud and clear.

You've been warned.

"Who's it from?" Casey asked.

"I'm not sure. It's a blocked number, probably a burner phone anyway," I looked at the message. "But I think it means we might be ok."

"Ok? How does a warning make us ok?"

"We're ok, if we stay out of their way."

I flipped the phone around to show her the simple text. Her eyes moved across the screen, and she shook her head.

I didn't know if the Triads were in the habit of sending random texts to people they considered a threat but so little made sense at that point. It could've been an overthinking mind, but part of me wondered whether Sergio Costa might have had something to do with it.

"You know, if I was to make a suggestion," Casey said, "and this is just me thinking out loud, but if you were ever going to consider a new line of work, maybe now would be a good time to make that decision."

It was Casey's way of telling me to back off in her own subtle way. She was right. This concerned her too, and right then, things felt like they were spiraling out of control for both of us. I could make my own decisions, yes, but she shouldn't have been put in the line of fire, and that was on me.

I needed to put her mind at ease. This case was not worth the price it was starting to cost. Mark Costa's laptop, the footage, the thief—none of it mattered when our lives were at stake because a notorious organization was out looking for us.

"I'll go back to the office this evening and I'll organize to meet with Lee Chan and sort this out." I nodded to amplify my intentions. "I promise I'll fix this."

She believed me, although she remained cautious as I laid things out for her. We had very little choice, but I intended to do what I could to make peace with the Triads.

"No, I'm going to do it now," I picked up my cell phone again. "I'll call him now. There's no time like the present."

It didn't take me long to locate Chan. One phone call to the restaurant where I'd previously met with him was all it took. But when I asked to speak to him, the man answering the phone barred my way.

"Mr. Chan is a very busy man. No time for chit chat."

"Tell him it's very important. This is Jack Valentine. He might remember me from—" but that was as far as I got.

"You were asked to leave last time, Mr. Valentine. People who learn slow don't live long and happy lives." His accent sounded as fake as the front for the restaurant he worked for, but that was the least of my concerns. My temper was starting to fray.

"You tell Mr. Chan that attacking us on the Interstate this morning failed and I'm not about to—"

"Interstate?" the man said, but this time in a perfect American accent. "If Mr. Chan wanted you dead, you'd already be dust by now."

He hung up, leaving me listening to nothing but silence. I believed him, realizing that he was telling the truth. Despite never meeting the man before, nor having any reason to believe his words, I knew that what he just said was true.

Of course, it was the truth. The Triads were a lot

more organized than what we'd experienced that afternoon. They wouldn't have made the mistake of missing the first time, nor would they have enacted that very public display of failure. That wasn't how the Triads operated. How could I have been so stupid for believing it at all?

"It wasn't the Triads," I confirmed to Casey. "This was too public for them."

She didn't argue, as if she knew it was true as well. They didn't miss, and our attackers had missed twice in one day.

Within two hours, the repair shop called. They'd already fixed the windows. Casey thanked them, and then walked over to pick up her Mini.

While she was gone, my mind was abuzz with possibilities, wondering who'd been the one to order a hit on us. If it wasn't the Triads, then Sergio Costa had to have been behind the whole thing from the start.

The storage unit was empty, and I wondered whether he'd rented it simply to draw us out, to see whether it was him we were investigating. Or maybe he just wanted to scare us off the case.

The storage unit was a set-up, that was the only thing I knew for sure. Nothing made sense yet, but I wasn't going to stop now.

We were too close to the truth to walk away.

CHAPTER 24

THERE WAS an intensified mood between Casey and I that afternoon, edgy, and with just a light touch of traffic on the road, it made for a quick journey back to the office. I half expected the building to be burned down, perhaps fire-bombed through the afternoon to drive home another one of the 'messages,' but when we rounded the corner and found the building still standing, I felt a little more confident.

I drove her car to the office, but Casey didn't speak throughout the drive. Her hand was inside her bag the entire time, no doubt close to her weapon. She stared at every car that came too close, checked the mirrors constantly, and when we saw a motorbike zip past us, her jaw clenched.

As I parked in the lot next to the office, Casey stepped out of the car and scanned the lot. No suspicious characters nearby. No movements in the shadows. I looked at her and she nodded. We were silent as we entered the elevator and made our way to the fifth floor of the building.

"What if they're waiting inside the office?" Casey asked as the elevator doors opened. "Do you think it's an ambush?"

"There's only one way to find out."

I stepped out of the elevator onto the hallway

floor. Casey drew her weapon and kept it by her hip, both hands holding it tightly. I approached the door, leaned close, and listened for any sounds behind the door. When I heard nothing, I reached for the keys.

"Time to see if we die," Casey whispered.

"If we die, I want you to know one thing—I've never liked your large black jacket. It makes you look like a bowling ball."

"Really?" Casey raised her eyebrows. "You're making jokes now? What if there's a bomb in there?"

"Hey, at least we'll go out with a bang."

I swung the door open, and the office was empty. It was untouched, just the way we had left it. We walked in and looked around to make sure nobody was waiting for us and to confirm that nothing had been tampered with. Casey looked under the tables. I looked in the closets. Nothing. The message on the Interstate and the one sent to my cell was as far as the mystery attacker was going to go on this one. For now, at least.

"I'm going for coffee," Casey said, and before I had a chance to respond, she'd disappeared back through the door. I would've told her to wait, but knew she would've gone anyway.

I went to my office and sat, staring out the window for a few moments to reflect on the previous twenty-four hours. Things had taken a turn for the worse, but we were close, and I knew the man who would get things back on track.

I looked out the window, and the weather had become nearly perfect as well, transforming from the drizzle we had during our return drive, to streaming sunshine coming in through the window. If it hadn't been for the morning's turn of events, the afternoon could've been a pleasant one, and I might've even suggested we drink our coffee at the park again.

What I needed was a way to ease the tension for Casey. Even with my firm belief that Lee Chan wasn't behind the attack, I knew she wouldn't rest much easier, if at all. Plus, that didn't completely rule the Triads out of the picture, especially since they were now affiliated with Sergio Costa.

When Casey did turn up again, the sweet punch of coffee distracted me. There was just something powerful about coffee that always grabbed my attention.

"I don't even have a will," Casey said as she sat down in front of my desk. "Isn't that funny? When everything was on the line, I was thinking about what I've left behind for the rest of the world."

"Where there's a will," I leaned forward and smiled. "There are fifty surprise relatives that you never knew you had."

"Every time," Casey smirked. "Here we are, about to die, and you're still making terrible jokes."

"Just trying to lighten the mood," I raised my hands in surrender and smiled. "We can't be serious all the time."

As I finished the coffee and sat back in my seat, Casey turned the focus back to work.

"Now we have some unknown person shooting at us, and who knows when they're going to show up again," she said. "We have to keep our eyes and ears open, Jack."

"I don't think it's quite an unknown. I think it was Sergio Costa's people."

"Why would Sergio Costa put a hit out on us? What purpose does that serve? We certainly don't have the laptop."

I knew it was scraping the very bottom of the barrel, but I explained how he might have rented the storage unit as a decoy, whether for us, or even for Mark. I figured he had someone sitting on it, lying in wait for anybody that took the bait and came snooping around. That way, he'd know for sure if someone was checking on him.

"Perhaps he wanted to see who would take the bait and when we waltzed in, he had the surveillance there to follow us and give us a scare."

She shook her head at that, not in a 'no way' kind of way, but one like maybe she doubted the theory. "I don't see why Sergio would go to all that trouble. Isn't he more likely just to send goons to beat you up?"

She had a point. "Maybe it's about confidence. Knowing that he has them on his side, effectively working with him, maybe he feels a little more untouchable than usual."

"I doubt that man is lacking in the confidence department. Either with, or without, the Triads behind him," Casey said. "Do you think they're still a problem?"

"Not yet," I began, "but they will become an issue if we keep pushing it. They may not have had anything to do with today's drama, but that doesn't mean they won't come to back up their partner if a threat presented itself, and we are a threat. As long as we continue looking for the person responsible for the theft from Mark, and Sergio continues to be a suspect in that investigation, they will remain a direct threat to us. We can't discount that."

"I agree," Casey said, gazing out through the window. "Do you think that this could be what Mark

Costa had been hoping for all along?"

"Meaning?"

"I was just thinking about what you said at the start of the investigation. Mark Costa was a suspect. Maybe he wanted everybody looking at his father. Maybe he 'stole' the laptop himself."

"But losing his affiliation with the Triads? Crossing them? How would that fit in?"

"He could want out of the deal he made with them," Casey continued. "And most people don't walk away from deals with the Triads—but if his father takes over the service he'd been providing, maybe it lessens the blow a little, and well… it's still in the family. And you can't tell me Sergio wouldn't look out for his son to some extent? Maybe Mark saw this as the best way out of the deal, so he can walk away from it all to live the quiet life. Maybe he's bought a beach house in the Bahamas, and this is it for him. We could just be a decoy, and he set this up from the start."

"What if Sergio was—" I began before a new voice broke in, cutting me off and effectively ending our conversation in a nanosecond.

"What if Sergio what?" Sergio Costa said, standing in the doorway to the office like a summoned apparition.

CHAPTER 25

"SERGIO," I SAID, rising from my chair. "What brings you out here?"

He stepped into the office, his presence larger than life. I saw movement out in the foyer. I looked over Sergio's shoulder, and spotted his hired help taking a seat. There were two of them. They were both big and ugly. One might even call them thugs.

"I need to talk to you." Sergio was firm. He looked at Casey, then sat in the chair next to her. "You've got a good boss here. Knows his stuff. He's well informed."

"I know," Casey replied. She looked at me, and I nodded, our words going unsaid. That was the connection between us. Not only could we read each other's mind, but she had such an impressive handle on situations, that she often knew the right course of action, regardless of how sudden or surprising those situations were.

Casey rose, excused herself, and closed the door, shutting Sergio and me in the office. He watched her the entire way, tilting his head a little to get a good look at her butt. He was that sort of guy, and I expected nothing less from the old sleaze.

Casey exiting the room was a top-shelf move. What she understood, and I didn't need to explain to her, was that Sergio was the kind of man that would open up a whole lot more if he was sitting in a one-on-one meeting, male to male. He was old-school, and rather than fight it, Casey accepted it to help our case. If Casey had stayed, there was every chance that he would say what he came to say, then leave without giving us a shred extra. But leaving me alone with him? I might just get something a little more out of the conversation than Sergio may have expected.

Once he was sure we were alone, Sergio turned back to me, a grin plastered across his face.

"Fine piece of tail you got there, Valentine. Does she multitask?"

I stood.

"Settle down," he threw his hands out. "I didn't mean any offense to your girl. You don't need to defend her honor."

He leaned back in his seat, crossed one leg over the other, and considered me for a moment. He hadn't come to share information, not voluntarily anyway. He'd come to ask questions, to find the answers he needed in order to move back into the game he knew and loved.

His attempt at intimidation wasn't going to work on me and he knew it. While he may have enjoyed putting people on the spot, watching them squirm with his beady eyes, it served no purpose, especially here with me.

An old saying crossed my mind, and it was one I considered firmly in play as we sat staring at each other across my desk—he who speaks first, loses.

We were in a face-off, and the first one to cave would be the subservient one. I had no intention of giving in and could sit there for the remainder of the day. Sergio was the outsider and probably had better things to do that morning and thus gave up his advantage.

"I need you to confirm it's missing," he finally said.

"Missing?"

"The laptop. He lost it during the break-in. Tell me I'm wrong." His grin remained, but the sincerity of his tone was quickly waning. He came to get the confirmation he needed, the one that would mean he was free from his son's blackmail. "That's why you came snooping around asking questions. That's why he hired you in the first place. Before I make a big move, I need you to confirm it."

As if to drive his point home, Sergio stood and slowly began to pace back and forth before me, his eyes remaining fixed on mine.

"If there is one thing I know about my son Marco, it's that he values very few things in life. He has always been the kind of person that could walk away from anything and not feel a shred of remorse or loss. There's not a sentimental bone in his weak body. And there's nothing in that apartment of his that he would consider valuable enough to hire someone like you to go and find again." He paused, held his hands out in a 'what-if' gesture, and added, "Except the footage on the laptop."

He was exactly right, but I wasn't about to give in to his questions. He was my number one suspect, although even that was quickly slipping through my fingers.

"Why did you send the motorbikes after us?" I fired back, wanting my own answers.

"The what?" he asked, squinting.

"The motorbikes on the Interstate. The riders

shooting at us this morning."

"Pal, I have got no idea what the hell you're talking about, but it sounds like you might have bigger fish to fry than little old me." He chuckled some, and I wondered whether it was part of the act or somehow the truth. "I had nothing to do with that."

"What about the laptop? Are you saying you didn't hire someone to get it back? Maybe you hired one of the security details inside the building to pay Mark's apartment a little visit while he wasn't around? It does sound like the smart thing to do."

"Perhaps, yes. But I hate to disappoint you, Jack. I didn't take the laptop, and I certainly didn't hire anybody to break into his apartment. I've looked for it before, but I never found it. Whatever is happening between Marco and I is between a father who failed and a son who took a few wrong turns."

"So this is nothing more than a simple family feud," I said, trying to sound as obnoxious as possible. "Just a father-son quarrel, so to speak. Because Mark was not behaving the way he'd been brought up to."

"Marco," he corrected me. "Marco is a prick of a man. If he wasn't my son, I'd have gotten rid of him years ago. But unfortunately, he's family. And that means I have to keep him alive, but it doesn't mean I have to like him."

"I can see how it may have spiraled out of control for you." He nodded at that and returned to his seat. I was getting through to him, slowly breaking down the barriers between us. It was the exact reason I needed Casey out of the room.

"Finding out that the footage is missing has been the best news to cross my desk in a very long time.

I'm glad I can finally have my company back. It's my company, I built that firm from scratch, and I was blackmailed out of it."

"I didn't say the laptop was missing," I reminded him.

"But you did," He laughed heartily at that. "If it wasn't missing, you wouldn't know about it. It's not exactly something that Marco announces to people." He clapped his hands together once and rubbed his hands. "I got what I came here for. Maybe not a direct answer, but enough for me to know that my hunch is right. Marco lost the laptop, hired you, and now is nervously waiting to see how I'll react." He leaned in a little closer. "Let me tell you how I'm going to react. The first thing I'm going to do is take back my business. It's time for Sergio Costa to return to where he is needed most."

I could feel his mood becoming much more talkative and decided to change tack again, maybe to get him into a more reflective mood. Men weakened in such a state, and I figured it might loosen his lips enough to spill something about the morning's attack. That episode was still burning brightly at the top of my list and I needed answers. In my belief at that moment in time, Sergio was my best chance to get them.

"Do you think you got away with murder?"

He retreated a little, and then raised his eyebrows, questioning if I really knew what was on the laptop. I nodded my response.

"The man got what he deserved," Sergio looked away. "He was a Building and Trade Union boss that was messing in my business. He was shutting my worksites down left, right, and center. We couldn't do a thing. Couldn't lift a finger on a worksite without his approval. Couldn't build anything and couldn't hire anyone. And he was doing it because of a personal vendetta against me. I didn't feel sorry for him. He had to go."

"You shot and killed a man and left him there to rot," I said, not bothering to sugarcoat his actions. "There's no statute of limitations on murder."

He got agitated then, perhaps finally sensing that I was baiting him. He stood tall, maybe to gain a little height over me. It wasn't enough.

"Take this visit as a friendly warning, Jack. Don't come any closer. I came here to get confirmation that the laptop was gone, and you gave that to me. Now I'm going to return home and start building my way back into a business that I started. And if you and your fancy tail back there decide to come after me, then you'll have some new friends of mine to deal with."

It was a threat, direct and to the point. He'd had his moment of reflection, but that was over. Sergio was feeling back on top, and our time to talk was finished.

"Whatever business you have with my son, consider me separated from that. I'm not your focus here, and if you don't back off, then people may get hurt. You know who my friends are, Jack." He glared at me. "You need to protect yours."

He didn't bother waiting for me to respond. He left the office, leaving his threat still hanging in the air.

CHAPTER 26

CASEY ENTERED my office moments after Sergio and his heavies had exited.

"Did you guys talk about baseball?" Casey said as she came back in. "Maybe you were chatting about the Cubs' chances this year? Or about how Sergio could've pitched for them if it wasn't for his shoulder?"

"Not quite. He suggested that if we continue to pursue him, he won't be as welcoming next time. And he let me know that he's good friends with some very dangerous people. We have to step carefully."

"But did you get anything worthwhile from him?"

I filled Casey in on the things she missed, the conversation about Mark and Sergio's next move. She listened as I relayed the chat as best I could, including the finer details about the night of the murder.

"Was he behind this morning's chase?" Casey asked.

"I don't think he was behind the attack." While the thought had plagued me for more than a few hours, it'd become clear that not even Sergio knew about it. There was something off about the whole thing. "I asked him outright, and he didn't have a clue what I was talking about. And I don't think it was the Triads either."

"Someone's trying to kill us," she said. "Maybe it

wasn't tied to this case? You do have a habit of making people angry. And it wouldn't be the first time someone waited a while before their anger became too much."

"I…" I was about to confirm this with Casey when something suddenly struck me. A random thought came to mind, and it needed my undivided attention. She saw my expression change in an instant.

"Jack, what is it?" Despite hearing her ask the question, my thoughts were in too deep to answer. My mind had gone back to the conversation I just had with Sergio, a specific part that at the time had simply shot over my head.

"Jack?" Casey repeated. "What is it?"

She sat forward and waved at me before I had the presence of mind to respond. When I did, a light-bulb went off in my head.

"It was something Sergio had mentioned during our chat."

"What?"

"He said the man he shot was a Union boss that was causing trouble for him. He killed him because he couldn't get any work done on a development site. Michael Hoffman, remember? A Union boss."

"That's right. He was a Union boss." She tilted her head the way she always did when she heard something, but was trying to make sense of it as well. Then it dawned on her. "Didn't the cleaning woman say her father was a Union boss?"

"Lauren Taylor. The daughter of a Union boss. Right under our nose the whole time," I nodded. "We need her family details."

CHAPTER 27

"FIVE YEARS ago, Michael Hoffman died of gunshot wounds, near the location of Leroy's bar. A Union boss." Casey pulled out the file we had on the deceased man. She read over a number of lines before she stopped. "And here's the kicker—he was never married, but his long-term partner's name is on the file."

I rubbed my hand across my brow. "Go on. Lay it on me."

"Her name was Sandra Taylor," Casey nodded. "A quick internet search on Sandra Taylor show s that she has a daughter named Lauren. Lauren went by her mother's last name—Taylor. That's why we didn't make the connection before now."

Casey turned the file around and showed me the reports we'd gathered earlier. Several newspaper articles were amongst them, with a photograph of the unfortunate man who would become another victim of the notorious property developer.

"One father gunned down in the prime of his life. A hard-talking, no-nonsense Union boss," I shook my head as I read some of the articles. "He was a thorn in Sergio Costa's side. These articles show that a week before the murder, he was threatening to organize a strike, and by all accounts was holding the Costa's at ransom."

"It wasn't an accident. This was a targeted hit by Sergio Costa," Casey said. "And we now know who had the motive to steal the laptop. The cleaner."

"We need more information on Lauren Taylor," I said.

"I hear you," Casey said and returned to her desk.

I opened my computer and began to search some of my own databases, in particular, the ones linked to current murder investigations. One of my contacts had managed to get a direct link into the system almost a year ago, and the password had never been updated. While I used it as sparingly as possible, this was as good a time as any to take full advantage.

Within seconds, Michael Hoffman's cold case file opened up, showing a photo of a man in his early sixties with a crewcut, facial stubble, and brown eyes. This was the father that was taken from Lauren Taylor, and I could only imagine how that would have affected her.

I worked my way through the particulars of the case, such as any possible leads, suspects, known associates, plus anything else investigating officers might have found useful. There was just a single mention of Sergio Costa under known associates, but other than that, nothing. The police didn't know just how close they were to solving that murder, with the killer's name already sitting in their file. All they needed was the murder evidence, video footage that was now in the custody of the victim's daughter.

But perhaps, I reasoned, this was a murder they were never going to solve. Sergio Costa's dirty money had a way of working its way into a number of hands.

Casey came back into my office five minutes later, her hands filled with several folders and single sheets.

"Anything of interest?" I asked as she deposited her work on the desk, adding it to the previous material. She shuffled through some of it, settled on a single folder, and picked it out.

"One thing that proved quite interesting is her relationship with a Cooper Lam." She opened the folder in front of me and pointed to the sheet with a photo of a thirty-something Asian male. My suspicions rose immediately. "They've been dating for a few years and Cooper's last job was as a police officer. He was kicked out five weeks ago for breaching privacy protocol."

My ears pricked up.

"I thought that might get your attention. It looks like Cooper Lam had been accessing classified files without authorization. When his superiors found out about it, they fired him."

"Any mention of which files?" Casey shook her head.

"No, but I'll take a guess and say it was an old cold case."

I opened another webpage—it was the department of motor vehicles and contained the registration details, home addresses, and vehicle particulars for everyone in the greater Chicago area. Again, I had the access to the government site through a contact. I punched in the name Cooper Lam and sat back to wait for the results. I turned the laptop to face Casey, and her jaw dropped open as she read the details.

Cooper Lam had a motorcycle license, as well as two registered bikes. I wasn't exactly an expert on the subject, but I vaguely recalled seeing the distinctive lettering of 'Suzuki' on the pursuer's fuel tank.

After a bit more typing and probing, I brought up

a second file, this one in the name of Lauren Taylor. She also held her motorcycle license. While she didn't appear to have a motorbike registered in her name, her partner Cooper had two.

"They were the ones chasing us," Casey said. "A former cop and a cleaner protecting their asset."

"But how did she know about the laptop?" I tapped my finger on the desk. "How did she get that information? How did she know to target the laptop? Mark wouldn't have told her."

"And if Lauren did steal the laptop, then why hadn't she done anything with it yet?" Casey asked. "If she had a plan to hand the footage over to the police, then wouldn't Sergio Costa already be behind bars?"

I nodded. We had so many unanswered questions, and there was only one way to resolve them.

I walked to the corner of the room and grabbed my leather jacket. "It's time to get some answers."

CHAPTER 28

THE DRIVE out to the Lower West Side took twenty-five minutes. Lauren Taylor lived in a small apartment building, sitting just two stories tall, with two apartments per floor. The building was a quaint residence in a quiet street. I parked a little further up the road, close enough to have a decent line of sight. Once I was securely parked, we waited.

We arrived at five-past-five, and after we'd been parked at the residence for an hour, Casey made the wise choice to go get coffee. There was a 7-Eleven close by, and after a quick trip, she climbed in and handed me a freshly brewed coffee. I took a sip and felt the familiar afterglow.

"Anything yet?"

"Not yet." I shook my head. "Her motorbike is in the driveway, so she's home."

"Registration has lapsed. Hasn't been updated in a year." With a coffee in one hand and her phone in the other, Casey checked on the details. We stared at the building. "What are the options?"

"First, we need to confirm she's home," I looked at my watch. "And then we need to establish when she leaves. Then we go inside the apartment and have a look around."

"Think she still has the laptop inside?"

"My guess is yes. After all the trouble she went

through to get it, I doubt she'd leave it lying around anywhere else. She'd want to make sure it was kept safe in a secure location, somewhere she could always keep an eye on it."

"But why wouldn't she have gone to the police yet? There's proof of who killed her father on that laptop. Or perhaps she has," Casey answered her own question. "Maybe they're building a case against Sergio Costa right now?"

"Maybe," I said. "Or perhaps she took it to them, and Sergio Costa's contacts in the PD have made the evidence disappear."

"You think she's tried to turn it over to the police but hasn't had any success?"

"That's a very real possibility," I said as my cell began to vibrate. I had silenced it the previous night and wouldn't normally have answered it. Answering phone calls during a stakeout put you at risk of finding out information that diverted attention away from the case and I felt so close to solving this one, I didn't need any extra distractions.

But when I saw the caller's name displayed on the screen, I knew I had to take it, and as I turned the cell around for Casey to see the name, she nodded.

"Hello Mark," I said after touching the answer button.

"I need to know where you're at. I need that laptop." I could sense that there was a lot more to his call than just a simple catch-up. He was sweating, and my guess was that Sergio hadn't wasted any time in letting him know his intentions of returning to the head of the company.

"We've got a lead." I was blunt.

"Another one?" He grunted. "You told me it was

Mindy. I sent some men over there, and they ransacked her apartment. The laptop wasn't there, Jack. They didn't find any evidence of it. They turned her place upside down and didn't find it. So where are you now?"

I wasn't prepared to give him anything else. He hadn't been an ideal client and I knew that if I did give him information, he wouldn't hesitate to act on it himself. I also knew that if I gave him the details surrounding my current stakeout, he couldn't resist confronting Lauren himself in the hope of getting his property back, and that would leave us hanging high and dry.

"Can't elaborate on that." I hoped that was enough. I knew it wasn't ideal for him, but given the sensitivity around this latest development, I didn't need Mr. High and Mighty coming in and causing havoc. "We'll have an answer for you by tomorrow."

"Jack, I'm not fooling around. I'm not a client that you can mess with. I need information. There's so much at stake here." He lowered his voice for dramatic effect, emphasizing the word need like a child desperate for a cookie. "Now let me be more precise. I need the laptop. Now. No more delays." He dropped his voice even further and I could hear him pull the phone even closer to his mouth. "My father was just here again, busting my balls. He knows something's up and is shooting off threats about coming back to take things over again."

I could sense his desperation. The man was being harassed by a father he no longer respected and the thought of losing the helm to his crystal palace seemed incomprehensible. Mark Costa wasn't going to give up without a fight, with or without the laptop in his possession, but his ship was taking on water, and he knew it.

"I can't give you what I don't have yet." I tried to sound calm, but in all honesty, I didn't respond well to that kind of pressure.

"You bring me the laptop back by tomorrow afternoon, and I will gladly double your fee. No questions asked. Bring me the laptop by tomorrow and your fee is doubled. I hope that motivates you to be more aggressive. If you need muscle to back you up, you let me know. I know the right guys that can break into anything."

There was desperation in his tone, the kind I often heard when squeezing guilty people for answers. Mark was no different, a guilty party to his own crime.

I was about to end the call when he slipped in a new question.

"Where are you?"

"I'm in the middle of something and we can't do it with interruptions."

"A stakeout? Let me sit in. I can help."

"No, you can't." There was no way I would give him even the slightest hope of joining me on this. "Not now."

"Who are you watching? At least give me that."

"No." I was done with him, and his words were becoming beyond desperate. I certainly felt like I owed him exactly zero of anything.

"I hired you and that means I own you."

I considered hanging up then, silencing him for the time being and giving Casey and me a chance to continue on undisturbed. But I hesitated just long enough for Mark to give me a final acknowledgment, to avoid making him angrier by hanging up on him.

"Ok, Jack, I'll wait." He ended the call, and I dropped the cell onto the dash.

Casey looked at me and shook her head. She'd heard everything. I had turned the earpiece volume up enough so she could hear the call and it saved me from needing to go back over things.

"Didn't take Sergio long to get the ball rolling," I said, returning my attention to Lauren's building. "He moved quickly."

"That doesn't surprise me. I'm astonished he hasn't already retaken his seat. Think Mark has a day before Sergio will throw him out?"

That wasn't something I had considered up to that point. How would Mark react if his father forced him out, before I had a chance to retrieve the laptop? Now that the possibility had been raised, the prospect refused to leave my mind.

I looked up and across to the building again, wishing there was some way we could see inside. There was a longing inside me that hoped Lauren would walk out, just to let us know her presence. But the longer I stared at it, the more I knew that it wouldn't happen, feeling as if I was watching and waiting for a pot of water to boil.

A motorbike tore up the street, the rider pushing the bike to its limits before decelerating with the same velocity. He had come up behind us, passed my pick-up and slowed enough to pull into the small parking lot in front of Lauren's building. Lauren emerged from the front door of the building.

We watched in silence as the rider first turned his bike off, lowered the kickstand, then gingerly lifted his other leg over the seat. From where we sat, the leg appeared to have suffered some form of trauma, it had been patched up, a black brace stretching from the very top of the leg all the way down to the ankle.

"It was them," Casey whispered as we saw the pair hug. It had come to her at exactly the same instant it did me like a great big curtain pulled back on the screen. Our attackers stood right in front of us.

"Would Mr. Assassin please stand up," was my reply as the rider removed his helmet.

Just as I had suspected during the chase, the man was in fact Asian, which is why I mistook him for being part of Lee Chan's crew. Now, as I sat there watching the couple embrace, the error of my thinking came back to haunt me.

"It had nothing to do with Chan or Sergio Costa," Casey said. "It was her all along. She's the thief, she's the attacker, and she's the problem."

"And now it's time to end this."

CHAPTER 29

LAUREN TAYLOR and Cooper Lam talked for a few moments on the front steps of the building before Cooper Lam worked his way back onto the bike, and once he had his helmet back on, he kicked the bike to life and disappeared just as fast as he'd arrived. Lauren watched him until he left before also disappearing back into her building.

We were alone again, sitting in the pick-up with a suspect barely a hundred yards from us. Time felt as if it had halted. Our investigation was left suspended in mid-air as the world continued all around us.

"This has turned into a righteous mess," I whispered.

"How? We have the break we needed. The laptop is right there." Casey looked at me from her seat. "All we need to do is get past those two violent bike riders and get into her apartment, and then we solve this."

"But do we want to give it back to Mark Costa, knowing what's on it?" I said. I knew the answer—it was a clear no, but we'd been hired to do a job. "Do we pull the pin here and leave the money behind?"

"Not yet. If it wasn't us, then Mark would just employ another investigation agency to find that laptop. And no doubt they'd come to the same conclusion we have. And if Mark gets word that she has the laptop, he'll kill her to get it," Casey shook her head. "I get the apprehension, but we don't even know where the laptop is yet. Let's confirm its whereabouts before we make any decisions on our next steps."

"I think if I hadn't been so distracted in the beginning, I could've avoided a lot of the drama that ended up in our lap. Lauren was right there in front of us the entire time. I mean, she was even there when we were walking into the crime scene, Casey. She was right there, and we didn't see it." I felt my temples thumping with anger. "She had access, ample opportunity, and with time, we would've found out her motive. All it would have taken was for me to take my tunnel-vision glasses off for a moment to look at all the suspects."

I was angry with myself. No, more than angry. I had almost gotten Casey killed because of my failures. But sitting there crying over spilled milk wasn't going to change anything, and looking for self-pity would only cost me more time. I looked back out to the building and knew what had to be done.

"We have to get her out of there somehow," I said. "What's the best way to drag her out?"

"Want me to go in and invite her out for a drink?"

"No, that would be too suspicious. She's a thief, and she knows we're investigating her crime. She'll be very cautious right now." I thought for a moment, then came up with a plan. It might not have been a perfect one, but given the situation and the complexity of it, I felt it was a better choice. "I'll call and get her to meet us at the office, and we won't be there. If she's cautious, then she's going to want to know what we know. I'll give her a story about how I think it's the security guard, Ivan Pushkin, and how she can help us investigate him."

"And then while she's out," Casey pointed towards the building, "it'll give us enough time to get inside her apartment and take a look around. If that laptop is inside, perhaps we can end one aspect of this case right here and now."

Casey nodded, and I reached for my cell. This would need to go smoothly, and I hoped that Lauren would take the bait. We hadn't talked to her in days and she hadn't yet realized that we were onto her, but I imagined she'd still be nervous. I thumbed in her number and hit the call button.

The phone began to ring and ring, and I listened with bated breath for her familiar voice. But after going through a dozen or so rings, the call simply dropped, with not even a voicemail message to greet me. I hit the end button and held the cell in my lap.

"No answer," I said, stating the obvious, more out of frustration.

"Maybe she's in the shower. Give it a minute and try again."

I nodded, and watched a Toyota pass us and held the cell steady. Five minutes later, I tried again, repeating the same process as before. The phone again began to ring, once, twice, three times. Five rings. I was just about to end the call again when she answered, her voice sounding a little out of breath.

"Hello?"

"Lauren. It's Jack Valentine. I'm the investigator helping Mark Costa. We spoke the other day at Walmart."

"Oh, yes," she replied, and I didn't sense any hesitation whatsoever. This woman had amazing self-control. "Sorry, was in the shower."

"I know it's after 6pm, but I was wondering if you could come down and meet us at my office? There were a few things I really need more information on. We've got a lead on the security guard of the building, Ivan Pushkin, and we'd like to talk to you about his recent behavior. We've got an office in the Loop, if you could make it in tonight?"

"For sure." Again, no hesitation. I wondered whether she was just completely clueless and perhaps we had again assumed incorrectly, or whether she was amazingly in control of her emotions. "You'll have to give me a bit, though. My motorbike is in the shop. I'll have to catch the train, so I won't be there until after 7pm. Is that ok?"

"Perfect. I'll text you the address."

"Cool. I'll see you soon."

She ended the call immediately, leaving me listening to nothing but silence. But my senses had been heightened and I was sure I detected something in her voice. Was it confidence?

Casey and I again sat patiently as we bided our time. Given our previous meeting with her, I knew that the woman liked to get her make-up just right and if she'd just gotten out of the shower, it might take her some time to apply.

Casey and I began to build a plan for when we entered the apartment. Casey found the apartment floor plan on a real estate website, and we studied the photos—one bedroom, living area, and a bathroom. A small kitchen and not much storage space. Time would be limited, especially once Lauren turned up at the office Downtown to find it locked. She might even catch a cab back, knowing that we sent her on a wild goose chase.

But the trap was set and we were ready.

It took Lauren just over twenty-five minutes to emerge from the building. She'd dressed in jeans, a t-shirt and a coat, with a white handbag slung over one shoulder. Her hair had been pulled back into a neat pony-tail, which swung side to side as she descended the steps and made her way towards the road.

Casey and I watched her go in silence. For just a brief second, I thought I saw her look directly at us.

We waited long enough for Lauren to make her way up the street and disappear around the corner towards the train station. Then, we waited another five minutes just to be sure she was truly gone. People had a habit of forgetting things, and having Lauren return for her wallet just as we were in the middle of breaking into her apartment would not have been an ideal situation. I preferred to stay on the side of caution when it came to breaking and entering.

Once we were sure she wouldn't return, Casey and I jumped out of the pick-up and casually walked up to the building's entrance. Casey had a piece of paper in her hand, a single, unfolded sheet. People generally saw others holding something in their hands as having a purpose. Nobody looks twice if a stranger has a purpose. A clipboard, a sheet of paper, even speaking on a cell make for the perfect disguise.

There was a mother and child standing in the foyer of the building and the mother simply waved at us with a warm smile before heading out into the sunshine. We continued on up the stairs until we were standing outside Apartment 5 on the second floor.

I briefly paused outside the door, Casey standing a little behind me. There was another apartment entrance at the other end of the corridor, and I looked down towards it, carefully listening for any sign that the occupant might be on their way out to greet us.

Once I was sure that the coast was clear, I turned back to Casey for a final nod of confirmation. She gave it, and I reached into my pocket for the kit I had brought with me. A second later, I was down on one knee, my lock-picking skills working their magic and an empty apartment waiting for us to explore.

Time was ticking, and we had to act fast.

CHAPTER 30

LOCK-PICKING was one of my better skills, and the door's simple barrier stood no chance once I went to work. It took barely a minute for me to slip the tumblers into place, and when I turned the knob, I felt the rush of a minor victory. We were in.

Casey carefully closed the door to the apartment behind her, locking it again, giving us the privacy needed for this little operation. Just as we'd discussed in the pick-up, our game plan was put into action the moment we were alone, with Casey heading for the bedroom while I remained in the living room.

I tried to imagine all the possible places where she would hide the laptop and those two rooms seemed to be the most obvious. The living room wasn't huge and had limited furniture, with a standard two-seater couch, two armchairs, a bookshelf, a TV cabinet, and the kind of coffee table that had a retractable lid to store little knick-knacks and magazines in.

I heard a noise outside the apartment door. I froze.

The door of the apartment across the hallway opened and closed. I stepped closer to the apartment door and listened for any further noises. There were none. I continued.

I searched the couch, carefully lifting the cushions and running my hands between the seats. Within a second of feeling my way along, I came across the first bit of treasure, a quarter, lost between the seats. I pulled it out, held it as I finished the sweep in that part, then returned it. It was crucial that everything was left exactly the way we had found it.

Once I finished the couch, I moved to the armchairs, starting with one and then the other. Each one proved fruitless, and I was about to move on to the next item when Casey interrupted me.

"Check these out," she whispered.

She was carrying a book, and when she stood next to me, I saw it was a photo album, opened to where a smiling Michael Hoffman was holding the much younger Lauren in his arms. They were looking at each other and in one hand, Lauren was holding a teddy bear. It was one that I'd already spotted in the brief time we were in the apartment.

I pointed to the teddy bear, then to the bookshelf where it was sitting beside a bunch of nondescript paperbacks. It looked almost as fresh as the day the photo had been snapped.

In the photo, the two were standing on a beach.

Casey flipped over to the next page and there was one of the young woman sitting at a table, a birthday cake waiting before her with numbered candles lined up and ready for her wish. It was her 21st and the night looked to have been filled with celebration. There was a crowd of people standing behind her, including a doting father who was leaning over to get closer to his daughter. The group had posed for the photo just long enough to snap the picture. It was at least fifteen years old, from a time when people still used cameras to capture moments.

"We've got to hurry," I said. "We don't have

long."

Casey nodded, took photos of the photo album pages with her cell phone, and returned to the bedroom. If we didn't find the laptop, we could review the photos once we were back at the office.

I walked over to the bookshelf, the teddy bear now holding new meaning for me. As I reached for it, part of me expected the laptop to slide out from underneath it, or perhaps to be simply sitting behind it, as if the iconic guardian had been given the task of watching over the invaluable possession.

But the moment I lifted it from its vantage point, I knew that the item I was searching for wasn't to be found in the bear's vicinity. It was lightweight, with nothing but an empty shelf behind it. After giving it a brief glance, I returned it and rifled through the rest of the items on the shelves.

There were a bunch of paperbacks, and I pulled each one out, looking behind them. On another shelf were several hardcovers but nothing behind them.

Down on the lowest shelf was a basket filled with random knick-knacks, and I felt my way through, finding nothing of interest. I grabbed a chair from the small dining set, sat it before the bookshelf and stood on it.

Sitting on top of the unit was a backpack that had been laid flat. I hadn't seen any indication of it lying on top and felt my heart quicken as I lifted it. It felt like the perfect place to hide the laptop, made even more plausible by the way it had been flattened, to hide it from prying eyes.

There was some weight to it. My conscience told me to be subjective, but I couldn't contain my excitement, stepping down and carrying the backpack to the couch to investigate it further.

The backpack had two main compartments and when I pulled the first zipper back to reveal the contents, I found it empty. But what I did feel was something hard and squarish in the adjoining compartment. Feeling my breath catch, I pulled back the second zipper.

Lying in the bottom of the compartment, and staring back at me with an air of contempt, were two textbooks, the kind that millions of students carried around with them throughout their studies. I briefly pulled one partly out, stared at the title, then dropped it again with disgust.

I returned the bag to where I had found it, picked up the chair, checked the underside, and returned it before I started to lose my cool.

I felt the sting of failure as the apartment refused to divulge its secrets. It was frustrating. Time was ticking. We'd already been hunting for more than ten minutes and we were running out of options.

The coffee table was next. I pulled back the top to reveal the contents inside. It was the last place I expected to find anything, given how accessible it was to anybody that came to visit, and after pushing a few items back and forth, it confirmed my suspicions.

After closing the top again, I tilted it slightly away from me to make sure the laptop wasn't taped underneath. It wasn't, but I remembered the other chair and dining table and returned to them. No treasure dropped for me there either, and I stood back for a second time.

For a moment, I wondered whether she might have given it to Cooper to guard, maybe she even gave him the laptop during their recent interaction.

But I doubted it, given her tragic personal connection to it.

It had to be in the apartment. It had to be. The laptop was too valuable to leave anywhere else and I knew that Lauren wasn't the kind of person to leave it lying around.

That was when another thought crossed my mind. What if she had it on her person? Maybe it was so valuable to her that she didn't trust leaving it anywhere, carrying it with her wherever she went. That was a distinct possibility, but I wasn't prepared to entertain that theory quite yet. I needed to make sure the laptop wasn't in the apartment before I went down that path.

I headed for the kitchen, itself a myriad of possibilities. This is where I used all of my intuition, searching through each shelf in turn. I looked through breakfast cereal boxes, ingredient canisters, behind random Tupperware containers, and a host of other items. In the fridge, I opened containers that might house the laptop. The freezer held a number of possibilities, and yet each of them failed to reveal the prize.

As a final act of desperation, I pulled the oven apart, checking several possible locations, including the interior.

I came up empty-handed.

I walked to the bedroom door and stood watching Casey for a brief moment. I wasn't so much watching her as I was running through the possibilities in my mind.

"Any luck?" I whispered to Casey, but her reply matched my own demeanor, the pair of us struggling to make any headway.

Where was it?

Like so many bedrooms I'd been in, there was a large print hanging above the bed and I pointed to it. Casey was sitting on the bed going through one of Lauren's drawers. She turned to look, stood, and lifted the frame from the wall. I half expected a door to a safe to be revealed, but the wall was blank.

I returned to the living room and spotted two more frames hanging on opposite walls. But as I removed each, there was nothing but cobwebs and a bare wall behind each. Our possibilities were starting to run out and so was our time.

It was then that I spotted the couch and the armchairs again. I hadn't checked underneath them.

I pulled the first armchair back and looked underneath. The bottom of the chair had been sealed with a thin fabric, stapled around the edges to keep it taut. The second looked the same, perhaps a little looser than the first. One of the edges was a little frayed, but not enough to hide what I was searching for.

The couch tipped easily, and I pulled it back far enough to lay the back of it down onto the floor.

I walked back around to inspect the underside and felt my stomach drop in an instant. There, on one side of the thin fabric, was a hole. It looked fresh; the edges still taut enough to hold the rest of the covering off the floor.

"Casey," I whispered, feeling the air turn electric.

She came in, saw what I had been doing, and walked around to my side. We stood there for a split second as realization set in, and after looking at each other for confirmation, I leaned down and reached inside.

I felt a messenger bag resting between two timber supports. It'd been locked into place with some sort of adhesive tape, and I worked my fingers around to pull it free. When I felt the final piece of adhesive give in, the bag slid free, and I carefully pulled it out.

The moment had arrived. I was anxious to get the thing open.

As I set the tan-colored bag down on the coffee table, I heard the door open behind me. When I turned to see who it was, Lauren greeted us with a snappy wave of the handgun she was holding.

"Find what you were looking for, Mr. Valentine?"

CHAPTER 31

"PUT THE couch upright and take a seat," Lauren's tone was firm. "And let's have a chat."

Given our current dilemma, I had no choice but to comply. I would've anyway, regardless of the circumstances. I needed information, as well as the laptop, and she was the only person who could satisfactorily add the missing pieces I needed to close this case.

After setting the couch upright again, Casey and I took our seats and watched as Lauren pulled one of the chairs from the kitchen area, setting it down on the other side of the room to give herself plenty of reaction time in case one of us tried to rush her. She kept the handgun pointed at us.

The tension in the air was thick enough to cut with a knife. Both Casey and I knew Lauren's involvement in the case, but something told me this woman wasn't acting out of malice. She was trying to find justice for her family and we were standing in the way of that. She didn't ask us to remove our weapons and put them on the table, which told me that she wasn't an experienced criminal nor a cold-blooded killer.

"I'm sorry for trying to hurt you on the Interstate," she began. "I just wanted to scare you guys, nothing more. I didn't know Cooper was going to pull a gun. He can be unpredictable like that. He's

211

a lot more aggressive than I am. If he was here now, he would've shot first and talked later."

At least any remaining questions about the interstate chase were answered. It was a small weight off my chest knowing that Sergio's new associates weren't behind that incident.

"Why were you so desperate for this laptop?" Casey asked.

"It has evidence of an unsolved crime." Lauren smiled a little. "Sergio Costa murdered my father and that laptop holds the evidence needed to convict him."

She reached forward and picked up the bag off the table, holding it almost as if it was her child.

"How can you be so sure that it was Sergio Costa?" Casey was gentle in her approach. "That's a strong accusation to make."

"It's not an accusation. I know it was Sergio Costa because Leroy Temper told me. He was there the night my father was murdered." Her hand gripped the gun tighter. "Nobody else knew what happened that night and when he finally told me, he explained it in far greater detail than I could've imagined."

Lauren stood and began to pace, the way people always did when they were trying to calm their nerves, redirecting their built-up fury into a calorie-burning release.

"I wasn't always a cleaner, you know?" She pointed the gun at us again. "At one time, I worked down as a barista near Leroy's bar. Leroy would stop by each night for a coffee and a chat. He knew my father, and they were old friends. Last year, Leroy told me the truth." She looked over to the bookshelf and the teddy bear that was there. She looked at it longingly for a long time before speaking again. "Sergio Costa stole my father from me, and I will do everything in my power to make sure he faces the justice he deserves. The last thing my father deserved was to be shot like a dog in the street and then left there to die. My father deserves justice, and that laptop will deliver it."

She gripped the gun tighter.

"But how did you know?" Casey said. She was buying time while I figured out our next steps. "How did you find out it was Sergio Costa and not some random shooting?"

"After years of not knowing, Leroy told me the truth. He used to come into the coffee shop, always with a smile on his face. In the days after the shooting, he changed. I only lasted a month at that job after my father died. I couldn't work on the same street where my father was killed." She shook her head. "Over twelve months ago, Leroy sought me out. He called me and asked to meet. I didn't know what it was about, I thought he just wanted to catch up, but he walked in a different man. He looked broken. He was racked with guilt about what he did, and it finally broke him. He told me everything. How he heard the gunshot, how a bloodied Mark Costa came into the bar, how he was offered so much money to sell the footage. Leroy kept his mouth shut for years but then said he was going to the cops, but he wanted to tell me first. He said he hadn't slept in years. The guilt broke him."

"Did he go to the cops?"

"He said that he was going to report it to the police and make a full confession, but that was the last time I heard from him. He didn't make it through the night. I don't know whether he actually made the report, all I know is that the next day, I heard that he was killed by a random drive-by shooting. There was no evidence that he ever went to the cops, but I don't think that the timing of his death was a coincidence."

She pulled out her cell phone and typed into it.

"Who are you messaging?" I asked.

"Cooper, my partner," she said. "He'll know what to do here."

She placed the phone back in her pocket.

"And he told you about the laptop?" I said, trying to buy some more time. Having another aggressor here would only complicate the situation. We needed to sort this out before he arrived.

"It was a horrible thing to hear," Lauren sat back down and leaned her elbows on her knees. "Four years after my father's murder, four years of not knowing who killed my father, Leroy came and sat me down and talked. He'd had a few drinks before I arrived, and he continued to drink well into the night. At one point, he began to confide in me, you know, just sharing bits about his business and how he was struggling to keep it under control."

"Bet he had quite the story to tell." Casey edged closer to Lauren as she listened, working Lauren with subtle hints so she would spill everything. It seemed to be working.

"He was a broken man. That was clear right away. He was heavy with a secret. I didn't know it at the time, but he sought me out to tell me that secret."

I felt her tense up a little and watched as she stared at the gun in her hand. She leaned back and rested the gun in her lap. She looked down at her hand to where a ring adorned one of her long and slender fingers, her eyes gazing into the distant past.

"What did Leroy tell you?" I asked, hoping for her to continue.

Casey edged closer again.

"Leroy told me he sold the footage that showed who killed my father. I was stunned. I remember my heart was beating so fast. I honestly thought I was going to pass out. Then he told me how Mark Costa had taken the only copy of the footage from that night. He paid him money in cash. Leroy said the bar was almost going bankrupt, struggling to stay afloat, and he couldn't pass up the money for the sale of the laptop." She shook her head. "But he didn't know. He didn't know the murdered man was my father."

"How did you know Mark Costa still had the laptop?"

"Because Leroy was dead the next day after he told me." She blinked back a tear. "He said that he was going to the cops with the story to try and end the nightmares that he had every night. He said it had weighed heavy on him every day since he sold the footage. And then Leroy told me that if he was murdered that night, it was clear evidence that the laptop still existed."

"Because if it didn't exist, then nobody could back up his story," I nodded. "Someone inside the police department tipped off Mark Costa, and Leroy ate a bullet."

She nodded.

"Why didn't you go to another police precinct?" A random thought had begun to stir in my mind, namely Wong and his endless investigations. "I'm sure they would have been eager for that kind of information. And the evidence," I added, nodding my head towards the laptop bag. "That would have been a deal sealer for sure."

"Are you kidding?" She shook her head immediately. "Leroy made it clear that the Costas still had contacts in the police department. He told me that if he turned up dead, then he would bet his life that Mark Costa still had possession of the laptop."

"And Leroy was murdered because he wanted to tell the truth."

"Leroy was troubled by what he did, and it got to the point where he had to expose the truth. After he was shot in a drive-by shooting, I knew I couldn't go to the cops. I had to find the evidence myself. It's taken over a year to get my hands on that laptop." She turned to me and nodded. "The Costa's reach goes a lot further than most people realize. Plenty of cops have had their pockets lined with Costa's money. I was just lucky I didn't have one try and take my statement. If they did, I might not be sitting here to tell you this story."

Casey edged closer to the end of the couch. She was within striking distance of Lauren now.

"So you got a job as a cleaner for Mark Costa's apartment building," I said, bringing her attention towards me.

"Not at first," she said. "First, I got a job as a temporary receptionist on his worksite, but I searched the place, and there was nothing. I was so determined to find this laptop. I did a little bit of poking around at his worksite, and I not only found out his address, but also that he had a company clean his apartment twice times a week. Wasn't too hard to land a job with them, either. All I needed to do was show a bit of cleavage to the pervert manager and I was in."

"Prestige Cleaning, right?" I asked.

Casey was ready to strike.

"Hired me on the spot, although it took a bit of time for me to get transferred to Mark's building. First job took me to the other side of the city, but eventually, I managed to get a transfer. Even then, it was a challenge to get to clean his apartment. Each cleaner has a certain section, specific floors, and specific apartments. It wasn't just a matter of transferring to the building."

"You bribed someone else?" I questioned, wondering to what lengths she had gone to find her father's killer.

"Not exactly a bribe, but a favor, nonetheless. Turns out that the girl who normally cleaned Mark's apartment had more than a few speeding tickets. I volunteered to pay them and she took the offer," she gave us a half-smile. "Once I got the job in Mark Costa's apartment, I spent ages trying to find the laptop. I've been cleaning his apartment for five months. He could've hidden it anywhere. Eventually, I discovered the safe in his home office. Then it all made sense."

"And so, you took it?" I said, pointing at the laptop bag.

"I got to know Ivan Pushkin, and he told me when the cameras were being updated. I staged the robbery to make it look like a random stranger had broken in. He stored it in a laptop bag, along with some cash in it, so I took all his cash from the safe as well. Found a bracelet intended for Mindy and dropped it into the corner of the room. I was hoping he'd find it there, or at least the cops would, but neither of them did. I was thinking of moving it again, but then you two showed up."

"And the cameras?"

"Ivan Pushkin had disclosed when the security cameras would be off, although I didn't tell him what I was doing." She shook her head. "But he also didn't sell me out after the burglary. He would've known it was me."

"You rented the storage unit," I said.

Casey turned to me, as if the question seemed ridiculous. When Lauren answered, her jaw dropped.

"Guilty as charged," she said. "I knew sooner or later you'd figure out that it must have been the cleaner. You turned out to be much more efficient than I'd hoped, and after running some checks on you, I found that I needed ways to throw you off my scent. The storage place was paid in cash, and I just told them that I worked for Sergio Costa, and they put his name on it. A bit of extra cash here and some cleavage there, and the handshake sealed the deal for the storage unit."

I recalled the fresh-faced employee talking with the truck driver that day. If he'd been the one taking her money, I doubt he would have put up much of a fight.

"And you still can't actually confirm whether your one piece of evidence is sitting inside that laptop, can you?" Casey relaxed. She pointed at the bag. "You can't get past the password?"

"Given the way Mark flipped out and then hired you, it left very little doubt in my mind that this was the one. Plus, when you eventually came calling, I had a feeling he'd lost what he'd needed to keep an upper hand over his father. I'm right, aren't I? It's on here."

I simply nodded.

"But accessing the laptop's contents has proven harder than I thought," she said. "It's password protected, and I've tried every possible combination Leroy might have used."

"I'm good at breaking passwords," Casey offered.

"No way. I'm not letting you do that. You've been paid to get the laptop back." Lauren squinted at Casey, moving the barrel of the gun to face her. "How do I know you won't just wipe everything that's on there?"

"You don't know that," Casey said. "But I don't see you having many other options. Where will you go? Who will you take it to? The Costas have reach in everything. If you take this to anyone, you run the risk of losing it."

"I'll take my chances."

"You won't get another chance," I said. "If you kill us, the cops find us here, and the Costas know it was you. If you let us walk, then the Costas know it was you. The only chance you have to open that laptop is sitting over here."

Lauren took a deep breath, held it, and finally exhaled slowly. She was nervous and scared at the same time. Now that the moment to actually reveal the truth had arrived, she wondered whether she would have the strength to push through.

She lowered the gun and set it carefully on the floor beside her chair before placing the laptop bag on the table in front of Casey.

Casey opened the laptop bag, removed the old laptop, and looked at Lauren. "Are you sure you're ready to watch this?"

She nodded. "It's time."

CHAPTER 32

PASSWORD CRACKING is a fine art.

It takes a little finesse, patience, and a small sliver of positivity to get through. Older computers were simpler to work over, given their limited capability. The laptop before Casey was at least ten years old, housing the kind of codes that made hacking into it a true art form. Her fingers typed faster than I could imagine as line after line after line of code flashed across the black screen.

"I'm breaking into the files via the safe mode of the computer," she explained. "We won't be able to access all the files on the hard-drive, and we won't be able to edit or download them, but we'll be able to access the larger files. If the footage from that night is located in a large folder, we'll be able to view it."

Casey sat with two sets of eyes staring at her, the room absolutely silent around us. Lauren still had her weapon trained on Casey as she typed. The laptop sat flat on the table, the room filled by the sound of her fingers typing and typing and typing. The occasional click here and clack there were enough to let me know that she was making progress, and when the black screen opened up to a series of folders, the laptop was prepared to give up its long-awaited secret.

"Date?" she asked as she scanned through the folders.

"Five years ago, 5th of May, after 10pm." Lauren said without blinking, staring at the folder. She stood and walked behind Casey, but remained a safe distance away.

Casey clicked on another line, typed more code, clicked it twice, and footage emerged of the back door to Leroy's bar.

"Want to do the honors?" Casey said, looking up at Lauren, waiting for her to press play.

She went to reach forward, then pulled her hand back. "No, you do it. I'm too nervous."

Casey slid the laptop towards Lauren, who simply looked up at me. I could see the terror in her eyes but knew this was important for her to do.

"Go ahead," I said, coaxing her a little. "This is what your father has been waiting for." That seemed to convince her, and her fingers carefully reached over and pressed Enter.

We watched and waited. The alley was empty. The footage was grainy, the lighting was dim, and there was no sound. At fifteen minutes past 10pm, a man appeared. He leaned against the wall of the alley, relieving himself next to the dumpster.

Only moments later, another figure appeared, and it was Sergio Costa. They talked before Mark Costa came into the screen, circling around them. He was scoping the place out.

There were two bright flashes but no sound.

Michael Hoffman fell to the ground.

Lauren's hand went to her mouth, and she blinked back tears. The two Costas looked around the alley, and then Sergio looked directly at the camera and pointed at it. Mark looked directly at it as well, and then he ran, presumably back into the bar to buy the footage.

"That was the moment," Lauren whispered. "They killed my dad." Her tears began to fall in earnest then, rolling down her smooth cheeks.

"This needs to go to the authorities," I said. "And quickly. If anybody finds out what this is, I don't have a shadow of a doubt they will murder you for it." I turned to Lauren. "Sergio Costa is in bed with the Chinese Triads now and they won't think twice about protecting their investment. If they know you have this, they'll do what they can to make it and you disappear."

"What about your money?" Lauren said. "Isn't that why you're here? To take the laptop back."

"Justice trumps money," I said. "I have a contact on the force. He'll know which precinct to take this to. You can take it yourself."

Lauren nodded, and I could see that she had the determination to see this through to the very end, regardless of the consequences. Casey left the laptop on the table and reached for the leather messenger bag which had previously held it. She picked it up and looked inside.

Lauren walked around the couch and closed the laptop, readying to place it back in the bag. Lauren's outstretched hand hung in the air for a moment too long as she waited for the bag, and I nudged Casey with my foot.

"The bag, Casey?" My eyes were still fixed on the laptop, and so I hadn't noticed anything else. When I turned to look at Casey, I saw that something else had taken her attention away.

Casey was looking into the messenger bag, one hand covering her mouth in a way that seemed to hide the shock of the moment.

I thought it was the footage that had taken her by surprise.

But in her hands, I saw a brief flash of something shiny.

She was holding a baseball card. It was a 1992 Turk Wendell card, where the picture was of the player brushing his teeth between innings. When she lifted it in mid-air, I saw the note attached to the back with a rubber band. The shock was instant. The note read:

For Rhys. The best 'real' brother ever.

It was short, to the point, and personalized the way only Casey could. Her hand came away from her mouth as her shaky tone tried to form the words fighting to come out.

"I gave this to Rhys the night he died," she whispered. "This is the last thing I ever gave him."

Time slowed as I tried to process what was happening. Shock turned to questions, and questions turned into a realization.

"Are you sure that's the card you gave Rhys?" I asked, but there was no need for confirmation. It was a specific card, made all the more unique with the personalized message written with it.

"He wanted this card so badly, and he'd finally been chosen to start for his minor league team. I wanted to say congratulations and thought this would be the best thing. I gave this to Rhys."

"I'm sure he loved it," I said, doing my best to

gain her attention. I tried to calm her down, reaching across to rest my hand on hers. "But it doesn't prove anything."

"I gave this to him the night he died," Casey whispered again. "He was there when Rhys died. Mark Costa had to be there. That's the only way he could've gotten this card. Mark Costa had to be there, Jack."

Despite the shock, I had to be the voice of reason.

"Ladies, we have to move," I said, rising to my feet. I could sense the danger and didn't want to waste another second. Lauren looked up at me, the laptop in her hands and a look of panic in her eyes.

"What is it? Cooper can meet us on the road," I repeated, gesturing towards the door. "We need to get out of here right now before it's too late."

"It's already too late," another voice said, and I looked up to see Mark Costa standing in the doorway.

CHAPTER 33

A LONG moment of silence followed Mark Costa's arrival at the apartment.

He was standing inside the open door; his Glock handgun pointed at us.

Lauren remained where she stood, the laptop held against her chest, guarding the precious cargo. She looked across the room, where her weapon remained. It was too far to dive for.

My weapon was still holstered, but any sudden movements would be met with Mark's aggression. He had the upper hand, and I didn't like it.

Casey sat off to my left, her hands held down in her lap, holding the card, her focus zoomed in on it.

I remained standing still, waiting for the new arrival to make his next move.

"Looks like you found my laptop," Mark Costa said, closing the door and locking it behind himself. He gestured for Lauren to take a seat next to the couch, then moved back even further, preferring more distance between himself and us. "Guns. Nice and slow, on the table."

Lauren gestured towards her weapon, still on the floor, on the other side of the room. Costa kicked it behind him. I raised my left hand, then slowly unclipped my weapon and placed it on the table. Casey didn't move, but Mark wasn't focused on her.

He stood near the kitchen, across the other side of the room, the gun held steady in his hand.

"I knew I couldn't trust you, Jack. You're built with integrity and honor, and I knew you'd turn on me once you found the laptop. I knew you couldn't resist the temptation to do the right thing." He turned his attention to the laptop in Lauren's hands. "And I can see I arrived just in the nick of time."

"How did you find us?" Lauren was breathless.

"Genius here." Mark pointed at me. "I placed a tracker on his truck, and it didn't take me long to figure out that this is where you lived. You taught me how to do it, remember, Jack?" Mark laughed. "I used the same type of tracker that you found under my sports car. An iPhone, and charger, set up with the 'Track My Phone' app. I got one of my staff to place it under your truck one night. I've been able to keep tabs on you the whole time. You were right, Jack, it was so simple to setup and so simple to use. As soon as I told you what was on the laptop, I knew I had to monitor you."

"Let them go, Mark. We can sit down and talk about this," I said, but he wasn't about to negotiate with me or anybody. He knew what Lauren held in her hands, and it was worth far more to him than anyone else could have offered. "Let's do this man to man."

"What did you do?" Casey whispered, the words squeezing between her clenched teeth. "What happened?"

I looked at her, surprised by her tone given the situation we were in, but I could see in an instant that the pistol sitting between her and Mark wasn't going to stop much.

Casey began to rise.

"Casey? How about you sit down again," Mark said, remaining where he stood. "Let's not complicate things. I paid you to do a job, remember?"

Casey stared at him and slowly lifted the card up high enough for him to see. Mark didn't appear to recognize what she was trying to show him, and he looked at me with confusion.

"Am I supposed to be guessing what that is?" he scoffed. "Is this some sort of baseball joke?"

Casey couldn't take her eyes off him, her face clenching as she tried to hold her rage in, aware that there was a much more sinister reason for the card to be in the laptop bag.

"Why was this in that messenger bag?" she managed to ask.

"I have no idea what you're talking about," he squinted as he pointed to the laptop. "I came here for that."

"This card had no reason to be in that bag," Casey continued. She took a step sideways, stepping around the coffee table. "You know what happened to him, don't you?"

Her voice was low, shaking with each word, trying to contain the grief and rage that was building.

Mark looked at her dumbfounded. He looked at me, held his arms to the side in a 'what the hell' gesture and said, "Help me out here?"

Casey took the denial as an attack, but I could see from the look on his face that he really didn't know. She flipped the card over and read the inscription out loud.

"'For Rhys. The best 'real' brother ever.'" Her jaw

clenched tight. "You were there. You had to be there when Rhys died. That's the only way you could've had this card. You know what happened to him, don't you?" she repeated.

He shuffled as something dawned on him.

"I'd forgotten that was in there," he said. "Wow. I was so caught up with getting the laptop back that everything else kind of slipped by." He looked back at Casey apologetically. "Forgive me," he mocked, a grin forming to replace the surprise.

"You know something," Casey spoke through gritted teeth. "What happened? You have to tell me what happened that night. You know, don't you?"

Mark considered her question before he scoffed again. "Who cares about the card? It's so long ago. Rhys got what he deserved and that's it."

Casey looked hurt, perhaps even a little confused. She shook her head, as if not wanting to hear those words from a man who had joined her in celebrating her brother's memory through the years, a man who had claimed to be Rhys's friend. She was trying to make sense of what she heard, and Mark had no intention of appeasing her in the slightest.

"You were his friend." the anger disappeared from her voice, replaced by shock. "You grieved for him, right there beside the rest of us when we buried him. You stood beside us. Was it all a lie?"

"He deserved what he got."

"Deserved what? To die?"

He looked at her, and I could see that he was struggling with her confrontation. He didn't want to be in that situation. He was supposed to be the one in control, and instead, it was Casey that was leading him.

"I'm here for the laptop, Casey, not some stupid little baseball card." Mark pulled back a little from her. "Which is the job I paid you to do."

"Your father killed my father," Lauren interrupted. "That's why you're here, isn't it? What are you going to do, continue protecting him?"

"Protect him?" Something triggered inside Mark, and it looked as if the words had rubbed him just the wrong way. "I'm not doing this to protect that old fool. This is so I can control him."

He stood taller, as if to reassert his authority.

"This laptop proves Sergio shot my father, and I'm taking it to the police." Lauren gripped the laptop. "He's going to jail. This laptop is the key to justice."

Lauren looked shocked when Mark began to laugh, a long and hearty laugh that seemed to mock her with every echo.

"You think you're hurting me by handing that in to the police? Lady, all you'll be doing is helping me long-term. Hell, I'll drive you down to the station myself. The sooner he's locked up, the quicker I can get back to my business."

"So why not give it to the police?"

"My father has so many of them in his pocket. Do you think he'll ever have a day in court? No chance. Not with his connections. Even if you find the right cop to take the evidence, my father will have that case thrown out before you can even think about court. This evidence is a threat, not the final nail."

Mark enjoyed being in control, and I realized that that was the only thing that truly mattered to him. He could've handed the laptop to the police years ago. He could've pushed for his father to be behind bars.

But he kept it so he could control and manipulate

229

his father.

"Mark!" It was Casey again, taking another step forward as she screamed for his attention.

We all turned back in shock.

"You have to tell me what happened to him." Her voice was wavering as the emotional grief simmered just beneath the surface. I'd never seen Casey like this, and it hurt me immensely to watch. She was hurting and nothing anyone did would heal that pain. She needed answers.

Mark stared back at her, and something changed in him at that moment. One minute he was in control, the arrogance that had driven him up to that point his main protection, but when Casey called his name with that pure grief driving it, something changed in him, as if a switch flipped to the on position. It was confession time, and he knew it.

He stood back, then stopped to look at Casey. Finally, he began to speak, and from where I was standing, it felt as if the entire world was listening.

"It was all the coach's fault," he whispered. "If he hadn't made the cut, then none of this would have happened."

"The coach?" Casey asked, her voice pitched with confusion.

"Coach Terry had pulled Rhys and me aside before practice that night and told us he needed to make a decision. Only one of us would make the team to play that weekend, and it was up to us to prove our spot to him." He looked directly at Casey as he said, "He made us compete against each other."

Casey stared in disbelief as she listened to Mark.

"The coach put us through our paces that night and we practiced our hearts out," he continued. "My father didn't want to let me quit, but there was no way I could pitch better than Rhys. He was going to the majors. And when it was all said and done, Coach pulled us aside at the end and gave us his decision—Rhys had won the spot, and I was dropped from the team."

"What happened?" Casey asked in disbelief.

"I never meant to hurt him," he said, grabbing at his hair with his left hand while the gun rested in his right. His breathing quickened, his face turning bright red as his own guilt was finally being released after a decade of deception.

"You killed him?" Casey mumbled, with tears starting to build. "You did it?"

"It was an accident," he said, locking eyes with her. "I never meant to kill him, Casey. He was like a brother to me as well." Mark's own grief now came through as the pair faced off, tears running down both their faces. "He was the only person I ever considered a real friend. He was the only person ever to like me for me. I didn't... I didn't mean to hurt him. It was an accident. He was supposed to just break his wrist."

"You killed him, didn't you?" Casey was shaking her head from side to side in disbelief at what she was hearing.

"I just wanted to injure him, Casey. I just couldn't face my father and tell him I'd lost my spot on the team. All I needed to do was put Rhys out of the game with a broken wrist. That's all I needed to do. We were drinking, celebrating his victory, and then I pushed him." He stared off to a faraway place. "But he fell too hard, and hit his head on the concrete path. I tried to help him back up, but he was all sluggish and… I panicked. He wasn't speaking and there was so much blood."

"You left him there to die," Casey's voice was rising. "You left Rhys to die."

"He had the card in his hand. He was so proud of it. I took it, maybe something to remember him by." He looked up at her again. "He was my friend, Casey. The only person I ever considered a friend."

Casey wasn't buying any more of his talk. Her anger had come to the surface. "You were never his friend. You murdered him; left him there like a dog to die alone! That's not what friends do!"

Mark pulled back then, trying to gain back control of himself. He was still in control of the room and retrained the gun on us.

"Enough of this. Give me the laptop and the card." His demand hung in the air for a long time before anybody reacted. He might've thought the gun was going to give him the protection he needed in order to achieve his intentions.

But the one thing Mark Costa hadn't counted on was a grieving sister and the lengths she would go to for justice.

CHAPTER 34

"CASEY." MARK Costa's voice was firm. "Don't come any closer, Casey."

His demand was met with nothing but silence. There was electricity in the air, a tension that was about to snap.

Lauren and I were passengers, looking on as all the attention turned to Casey and Mark.

Mark still had his gun trained on Lauren, focusing on the laptop, but Casey approached slowly from the left, snarling like a wolf ready to take its prey.

For a long five seconds, there was a pause in the room, each party resetting in anticipation of the next move.

And when Mark went to repeat his demand, it set off a chain reaction.

A low guttural scream began to emanate from Casey, and when I looked in that direction, I watched as Casey first tensed, then launched herself in Mark's direction. I expected him to turn the gun on her and fire, but there was no sound.

His face contorted in both surprise and fear as the crazed woman flew at him.

Just before Casey reached him, he held up his palms and deflected her attack behind him.

Casey was traveling way too fast to react and found herself unable to stop before crashing into the chair and falling to the floor in a tangle of arms and legs.

His gun was knocked to the ground, and Casey rolled over and tried to grab it.

Mark reacted first, grabbing the gun, and before anyone else could react, he jumped to his right, picked up the laptop, and didn't slow down as he jumped through the open window.

One second, he was standing there, the next, we saw him disappear beneath the window ledge.

I rushed to the window to see whether Mark had crumpled to the ground beneath. We weren't on the ground floor and the fall would have been significant.

But as I popped my head through the open window, I could see him lying in a garden bed, some bulbous shrubs breaking his fall and giving him an almost perfect cushion of foliage to land on.

I heard a commotion in the room behind me and as I turned my attention back inside, I watched Casey pull the door open and disappear out into the hallway. Another look outside and Mark was up on his feet, taking off down the street in a mad dash to escape his tormentor.

The chase was on.

Cooper Lam, the motorbike rider and Lauren's partner, appeared in the doorway. The confusion on his face was clear.

There was little I could do for Lauren, who was standing there in shock and confusion. My concern was the man running down the street and a sister's wrath close behind. I made a mad dash for the door and tried to catch up.

As I hurtled down the staircase, two steps at a time, the pain in my knees grew, an unnecessary distraction that I'd ignored for a long time.

I sprinted out the door and onto the sidewalk.

Within the first block of sprinting, the pain in my legs grew, my breath came in short sharp rasps, and I felt as if I was about to collapse in a coughing fit. I was sure that my lungs were on the verge of exploding.

Age has a way of creeping up on a person, and it has a multitude of hungry friends—the kind that robs a person of speed, agility, stamina, and strength. Age had a carnivorous hunger that was robbing me of the things I used to take for granted. During those first few steps of the chase, it was clear I was no longer the athletic man I used to be.

As I reached the street corner, I saw Casey disappear behind a parked car, turning down a side street. I swallowed as hard as I could, gritted my teeth, and continued.

I could almost smell the rage behind her, and I knew that there was very little chance that she would let Mark escape from this situation.

I continued running, doing my best to ignore the pain, but eventually, I reached the point where I'd lost sight of her. She'd turned down a long alley, and once I reached the mouth of it, I could see her sprinting along in the distance.

She had a decent head start on me, and I still hadn't seen any sign of Mark.

Perhaps he'd managed to evade her, maybe making it back to his car. But watching Casey sprint in that direction like a wolf who'd caught a scent of blood, I sensed he must've been close.

All I could do was try and keep up with them, running as fast as I could down that alley. A dog came bounding out from a rear gate, and my feet tangled up, sending me flailing to the ground. It yelped in surprise before sprinting back into its yard, leaving me to find my feet again.

As I resumed my chase, I heard a commotion from further down the alley. Voices were shouting and I could make out Casey screaming something about making him pay.

A silence followed and running that final fifty yards felt like the longest run of my life.

Time was effectively up. I needed to find the extra strength in me to close the distance.

The voice picked up again as I neared the opening to a little alcove in the alley.

I still couldn't make out where exactly they were, but the sounds of a struggle indicated they were near. I pushed my legs even harder. I rounded the corner and saw a tangle of arms and legs rolling around on the ground as Casey was wrestling with Mark in the distance.

The pair of them looked like a couple of Olympic wrestlers, fighting for different weight divisions. The laptop was beside them, dropped by Mark, and the gun was back in Mark's hand.

They were wrestling for control, but Mark seemed to be winning.

I sprinted closer.

They were both flailing about, an endless arm wrestle for domination, their hands fighting for control of the gun. I could see Mark's face flushed, dripping with sweat, as he desperately tried to snatch the pistol back long enough to aim it at his attacker.

But nothing was going to compete with a grieving sister who'd finally allowed a full decade of sorrow, anger, and outright wrath to come pouring out. Casey was bent on stopping him, a weapon of raw torment that had her nemesis within her clutches. Her time was now, and he wasn't going to stand in her way.

They rolled back and forth, the gun caught somewhere between their twisting and turning arms. Fingers were randomly snatching at the firearm, slapped away, only to retry grasping it again.

I didn't slow as I got closer, the vision of what lay before me coming into clarity within a split second. I was going to hit Mark with a shoulder charge from the depths of hell.

But just a couple of steps from them, an explosion ripped through the air, temporarily deafening me. The ringing in my ears gripped my every fiber, shocking me into freezing.

They stopped wrestling.

I stopped charging forward.

They paused to stare into each other's eyes.

Time stopped long enough for them to exchange whatever needed to be said without words.

Casey pulled back as Mark seemed to relax. He fell back on the pavement, staring up into the clear sky above. Blood started trickling along the concrete beneath, pooling beside him.

Casey never took her eyes off him, rising to her feet and hovering over Mark. The gun was still in Mark's hand.

For a moment, I thought it might have been just a graze, perhaps even a flesh wound, maybe just enough to halt him for the time being.

But a lot of blood kept pouring out. I passed Casey and fell to my knees, placing my hands over the wound.

The blood flow couldn't be slowed, the artery in his thigh releasing his life in a torrent of red horror.

It had accumulated in a small pool beneath him. I placed my jacket over the wound, pressing hard, trying to save his life.

A bystander dialed 911 and screamed for the paramedics.

Mark turned toward Casey and tried to mouth his last words. She might've heard them, I'm not sure. I did.

But his apology was far too late to have any real significance.

His face began to pale as he looked back to the sky, taking in the beauty one final time.

Mark Costa's final breath came with his eyes turned upwards.

The man had murdered her brother, blackmailed his own father for years, withheld vital information about the murder of Michael Hoffman, most likely murdered Leroy Temper, and now, he was gone.

Casey sat down on the sidewalk and waited for the inevitable interview she would need to give once the authorities showed up.

A minute after Mark had passed, Lauren Taylor and Cooper Lam ran around the corner and stopped short of seeing his body. Lauren walked over to Casey, dropped to the ground and pulled the grieving woman into her arms. Cooper picked up the fallen laptop.

The two grieving women sat embracing each other, their tears of both grief and relief finally able to fall freely. Their sobbing was almost silent as more people began to show up, and soon, there was a small crowd standing at the end of the alley.

The sirens sounded in the distance, and within moments, both paramedics and police began to try and make sense of the scene before them. And throughout it, the women held each other and let go of their pain.

Soon, the police came to me for answers.

They gave me a towel, and I wiped the blood off my hands. I tried my best to give them what they needed.

The paramedics treated Casey when they found she had blood dripping down her leg. It was worse than she first thought, adrenalin masking her pain. It wasn't long before she was whisked away in an ambulance.

The police talked to Lauren, and they took the laptop.

Once all the information had been relayed, there was no going back. No number of connections could save Sergio now.

And the man to thank was Mark Costa himself.

CHAPTER 35

CASEY SPENT the night in the hospital. The bullet that hit Mark Costa had also grazed the inside of Casey's thigh and she needed five stitches to mend her back up. I remained with Casey for as long as the nurses allowed that night and ended up heading home five minutes before midnight. We didn't talk about Rhys, not yet, but I could see the pain in her eyes.

From what I heard the next morning, the cops would clear Casey of any charges, noting that she acted in self-defense. Her finger wasn't on the trigger at the time of the shot, and Mark Costa had effectively shot himself while they were wrestling.

Lauren Taylor and Cooper Lam had come past the hospital the previous night, but only stayed long enough to thank us for our input and for finally putting an end to her ordeal. The laptop was now with the police and the case was too big to sweep under the rug. Lauren Taylor's father would finally receive the justice he deserved. I didn't ask about the money from the safe. I figured it was a small reward for her effort to find her father's killer.

Lauren looked like a different woman, as if a heavy weight had been taken off her shoulders. She'd taken her life back by force, fought and struggled against the powerful and corrupt, and was able to offer her family answers to questions they never knew to ask.

Cooper apologized for the attack on the Interstate, and we shook hands. They left, and I told them to ride safely.

After a night of restless sleep, I returned to the hospital, where I found Casey sitting upright in bed. The hospital gown was gone, replaced by jeans and a sweater, and when she saw me, she shared the news that she could go home.

"I'm free to go," she said.

"That didn't take you long."

"It's almost like…" she looked at me and smiled. "Like I'm 'Russian' to get out of here."

"That's a terrible joke," I laughed. "Where did you hear such a bad joke?"

"From a very terrible comedian." Casey pointed to me. "The police have been here all morning, and I've given them an official statement. Looks like I'm in the clear." She paused for a moment. "I'm sorry Mark Costa lost his life. I wish it didn't end like that." She sighed and paused for a few moments before her head snapped up. "So, boss, when's our next job?"

"Don't worry about work for a while," I said. "We might not have been paid the 50k for finding the laptop, but we're sitting pretty well."

"What else am I going to do?" she said. "I can't go chasing my life-long dreams just yet. I have to wait until I'm old and bitter like you."

"Ouch." I laughed. "It seems the bullet didn't dent your sassiness."

"No chance. That's part of my DNA." She sat on the edge of the bed, ready to move. "Ready to give a girl a ride?"

"Wouldn't have it any other way," I replied, grabbed her bag, and helped her up.

There was a set of crutches by the bed, but when I pointed to them, Casey jeered. "No thanks, I'll manage."

We walked slowly back to my truck, and after I helped Casey climb into the passenger seat, I ran around and jumped in.

"Home?" I asked, firing the beast up.

"How about a drink instead?" Casey suggested. "I think I've earned a shot from the boss."

"Too true."

As I was about to pull out of the parking lot, Casey reached over and touched my forearm. I looked at her and she appeared somewhat distracted.

"Listen, do you mind if we stop off somewhere first? There's something I need to do."

I listened to her request, nodded, and changed direction. I understood every word she said.

The detour took a little longer to reach, but I knew it was somewhere she needed to be. She had news to share, and Rhys needed to know that she had gotten justice for him.

When we reached the cemetery, I helped Casey out of the truck, but instead of following her, I hopped back in. This was something she needed to do alone, and I would be nearby if she needed me. She limped her way to his grave, then stood before him.

I didn't watch for the most part, feeling that they deserved some privacy. The couple of times I glanced in her direction to make sure she was ok; I could tell she was emotional while speaking to her brother. She took out the baseball card from her purse, kissed it, and then placed it at the bottom of the headstone.

It took Casey almost an hour to get through what she needed to say, and when she returned, I took us back out into traffic and turned towards the bar. We drove in silence for the most part. When we reached the parking lot of the Angry Friar, my favorite dive bar, I helped Casey from the truck before leading her inside.

We ordered a couple of Basil Hayden's, a sweet bourbon, to celebrate the successful case, although we both knew it was far more than that we were toasting to. As we held our glasses up that first time, I left it to her to speak the words. The toast ended up being just a single word, one that held just as much meaning for her, as it did me.

"Family," she whispered.

"Family," I repeated, clinked her glass with mine and drank deeply.

We sat in silence for a while, staring into nothing.

"Still think he sought us out specifically?" Casey broke the silence after a few minutes.

"I think he did," I said. "I think he forgot about the baseball card, and he wanted us to find the laptop. Although he didn't trust us, he knew we were the right people to find it. And the dirty dog was keeping tabs on us the whole time, tracking our movements, expecting us to choose honor over money."

"What a screw-up on his behalf," she said. "He managed to solve his own crime, help bring murder charges against his father, and fatally shoot himself in the leg, all in one week."

"Speaking of Sergio," I began. "As of this morning, he was officially on the run, although Detective Williams said that a disheveled looking man was picked up when his car broke down on the side of the road in upstate New York. The man just happens to match the description of a Sergio Costa, wanted in connection with the murder of Michael Hoffman."

Sergio had taken off the second he'd heard the news about his son. The police were hot on his heels and were in the process of bringing him back to Illinois to face charges.

"What about the Triads? Think they'll want to come get some payback for Mark or Sergio?" Casey asked.

"Not now that Sergio is going to jail. They'll consider Sergio Costa a loss, Mark Costa a write-off, and us as nothing more than a temporary inconvenience."

"Who would've thought that taking on Mark's case would end up with us solving two murders and putting Sergio Costa away for good?"

I raised my glass a second time, and we clinked again. As I took a swig, Casey looked as if she suddenly remembered something and reached into her handbag.

"That reminds me," she said, pulling out a small envelope. She held it out to me and waited for me to take it.

"What's this?" I asked, curiously. "It's not my birthday, is it?"

"No, but I thought you could use this."

I took the envelope and removed the small card that was inside. It was a gift certificate, printed out on a piece of paper, made out to me. I didn't initially see the joke, but when I saw her face, I slowly began to chuckle.

"A gym membership? Really?"

"With some personal training sessions thrown in," she laughed and pointed at me. "You really could benefit from working out. You've become a lot less fit this year."

I chuckled long and hard, amused by her gentle dig.

And I was sure that I'd need to increase my fitness level to be ready for our next case.

CHAPTER 36

THE FOLLOWING morning, the drive out to Claire's cemetery was a hard one, given the amount of tragedy that had surrounded my life the previous few days. Watching people struggle with their grief wasn't easy for me, not when I had my tragic past still tormenting me as well.

There was something else that made the trip to see Claire so difficult—she was continuing to fade from my life. Every time I realized it, every time I realized that I hadn't thought about her in hours, I felt sick to my stomach.

When she first passed away, there were a number of big changes, changes which one is forced to deal with, such as coming to terms with the fact that the person is gone forever, that you'll never be able to create fresh memories with them. At the start, when the grief was so fresh, she was always on my mind. When I drove to the shops, I thought of her. When I went to work, I thought of her. When I lay in bed at night, tossing and turning, unable to sleep, I thought of her. But now, as the years passed, she'd been continuing to recede in my memories, appearing less and less with each passing day, almost gone forever.

I hated myself for that.

I'd already lost her once, and I didn't want to lose her from my memories as well.

The agony was still there when I thought of her. There was that aching deep inside. People always told me that time healed everything but they lied. They said it would get easier as time passed, that somehow time was supposed to make the pain disappear, but who were they to tell me when the pain would subside?

The truth, I was discovering, was that the pain did anything but diminish. It simply changed, just like a deep cut on your hand. There was the initial sting, that fear, but soon the pain numbed, long enough for you to acclimatize to the wound. But it wasn't long before the throbbing would start, effectively replacing one type of pain with another.

Time healed nothing—it simply changed things.

I couldn't let death be Claire's final stanza. I had to hold on, to ensure that she lived as long as I did.

By the time I reached her grave and stood before her, I'd worked myself up into a lot of pain.

The rest of her neighbors were there, of course—Alicia, Melanie, Frederick. They were there, just like always, and so was my Claire. All of them spending their time resting in eternal peace.

I stood in front of her, said a small prayer and made the sign of the cross, just in case. Hope is what the religious people preached, and it was here that I truly believed. I had to. I had to have faith that my Claire was thriving in the afterlife. That faith saved me numerous times over.

I spent the next hour sharing events of the previous week with her, telling Claire about the brave woman who I worked with. I hoped Claire enjoyed listening to the details.

It wasn't all about talking and sharing war stories

with her. There was also time to reflect, time to sit silently before her and just experience the silence of her surroundings. The peace and tranquility of the place was perfect for our conversation.

With the sun on my back, sitting on the grass, I told her my best jokes I'd heard since we'd last talked.

"Claire, honey, I got a new pair of gloves last week, but they're both 'lefts,' which on the one hand is great, but on the other, it's just not right."

I swore I heard her laughter echoing in the distance.

"My friend Tim told me he had a secret," I smiled. "He told me he had multiple personalities. I hadn't heard that before, but he was being Frank with me."

I chuckled loud enough for the both of us.

"As I was driving to work, I saw a sign the other day that said, 'Watch for children,' and I thought, 'Yeah, that sounds like a fair trade.'"

It was overcast that morning, and as I sat there laughing at my own jokes, the sun broke free from the clouds, bathing the two of us in golden sunlight.

I like to think that it was Claire giving me a sign, to let me know that she was watching, laughing, or perhaps even right there sitting beside me. I have faith it was her.

During the time I spent with Claire that morning, not a single other person came into the area. It was as if fate had given me time and space to reconnect with my beloved. There were tears, of course, and perhaps that was why whoever was in charge had kept the others away for me.

When it was time to go, I stood, kissed her headstone, and wished her well, promising to return soon and to never let her memory die. Leaving her in that place was a bitter-sweet deal, but there was always more work to do, always another case to focus on.

I walked away from her that day, and it was one of the hardest walks of all.

Is death final? No, not a chance. Not even close.

<u>THE END</u>

AUTHOR'S NOTE:

Thank you for reading The Thief.

I loved writing this installment of Jack and Casey's story. This story was hard to write at times, especially when touching on sensitive subjects, but that's what storytelling is—drawing on my own personal experiences to create an authentic experience for you, the reader.

Thank you to Andy, Jessica, and Bel. Their help was greatly appreciated in getting this story to publication.

I've had a busy year—along with writing crime thrillers, two of my children have almost completed their schooling (and I'm immensely proud of them), I've completed further post-graduate study in criminology, and I've worked a number of contracts as a criminologist. It's exciting, but as another year comes to a close, I wonder where it's all gone? Surely, time is moving faster, because I didn't feel like that last trip around the sun was a whole year!

Positive reviews mean the world to authors. If you enjoyed this story, please consider writing a review.

I love hearing from readers, so if you feel like getting in contact, send a message to: peter@peteromahoney.com

Best Wishes,
Peter O'Mahoney

ABOUT THE AUTHOR:

Peter O'Mahoney is the author of the best-selling Tex Hunter, Bill Harvey, and Jack Valentine thrillers. As well as writing crime thrillers, O'Mahoney is a criminologist, and uses this knowledge and experience to guide his stories. He has a keen interest in law and is an active member of the American Society of Criminology.

O'Mahoney was raised on a healthy dose of Perry Mason stories—the pace and style of these books inspired him to write as a teenager, and he hasn't stopped since. He loves exciting characters, breathtaking plots, but more than anything, he loves a great twist. He has worked with various authors on plot design; including J.J Miller, Patrick Graham, and William Thomas.

His thrillers have entertained hundreds of thousands of readers around the world.

O'Mahoney splits his time between Chicago and the wide open beaches of Australia.

Website: peteromahoney.com
Contact: peter@peteromahoney.com

ALSO BY PETER O'MAHONEY

In the Jack Valentine Mystery Series:

Gates of Power
The Hostage
The Shooter
The Witness

*****

In the Tex Hunter Legal Thriller series:

Power and Justice
Faith and Justice
Corrupt Justice
Deadly Justice
Saving Justice
Natural Justice
Freedom and Justice
Losing Justice
Failing Justice

*****

In the Joe Hennessy Legal Thriller series:

The Southern Lawyer
The Southern Criminal
The Southern Killer